The Missing Manhattan Heirs

Long-lost billions, unexpected romances!

When billionaire Mark Hinton is declared dead, a search begins for his three long-lost children. These heirs must be found as soon as possible and flown to New York to claim their rightful inheritance.

Their new wealth will change their lives forever, but what these three siblings aren't expecting is to find the one thing money can't buy...love!

Meet the first heir Leni in

Cinderella's Billion-Dollar Christmas

Join the second heir Charlotte in

The Bodyguard and the Heiress

Both available now!

And discover the other heir soon!

Dear Reader,

Rule number one of being a bodyguard is to not get romantically involved with the client. As owner of the security firm guarding the heirs to deceased billionaire Mark Hinton's fortune, Jace MacDonald has always strictly adhered to that rule. Then he meets Charlotte Fillion, Mark Hinton's middle child. She's tall. She's gorgeous. And she's just about the most interesting person he's ever met.

Charlotte is funny and pragmatic. Just what the doctor ordered for Jace. But there's trouble coming in their lives. Surprises.

And sometimes love doesn't fit...

Or maybe it does and Jace needs to learn some rules are made to be broken.

I had a blast writing this book. I hope you enjoy reading it as much as I enjoyed getting to know Jace and Charlotte.

Happy reading!

Susan Meier

The Bodyguard
and the Heiress

—

Susan Meier

HARLEQUIN®

Romance™

Recycling programs
for this product may
not exist in your area.

ISBN-13: 978-1-335-55622-6

The Bodyguard and the Heiress

Harlequin Enterprises ULC
22 Adelaide St. West, 40th Floor
Toronto, Ontario M5H 4E3, Canada
www.Harlequin.com

Printed in U.S.A.

Susan Meier is the author of over fifty books for Harlequin. *The Tycoon's Secret Daughter* was a Romance Writers of America RITA® Award finalist, and *Nanny for the Millionaire's Twins* won the Book Buyers Best Award and was a finalist in the National Readers' Choice Awards. Susan is married and has three children. One of eleven children herself, she loves to write about the complexity of families and totally believes in the power of love.

Books by Susan Meier

Harlequin Romance

The Missing Manhattan Heirs

Cinderella's Billion-Dollar Christmas

Manhattan Babies

Carrying the Billionaire's Baby
A Diamond for the Single Mom
Falling for the Pregnant Heiress

The Princes of Xaviera

Pregnant with a Royal Baby!
Wedded for His Royal Duty

The Vineyards of Calanetti

A Bride for the Italian Boss

A Mistletoe Kiss with the Boss
The Boss's Fake Fiancée
The Spanish Millionaire's Runaway Bride

Visit the Author Profile page
at Harlequin.com for more titles.

For Selena Blake—brainstormer, blurb writer,
marketer extraordinaire...friend.

Praise for
Susan Meier

"I loved reading *A Diamond for the Single Mom*.
Susan Meier has once again made her characters
come to life...the perfect book to warm your heart."

CHAPTER ONE

"Go to Pennsylvania, they said…"

Jace MacDonald mumbled to himself as he walked through three inches of mud coating the little hills and valleys created by a dozen pieces of heavy equipment digging what looked to be a foundation for an enormous building.

"All you have to do is tell her she's one of the heirs to Mark Hinton's estate, get her on a plane to New York and keep her out of the public eye until her vetting process is complete."

His fancy Italian loafer sank into the unstable dirt as he took another step, and he groaned. Charlotte Fillion was a bigwig in some highbrow construction company. Yet when he'd called them for her location, they'd sent him here…to a jobsite.

Luckily, he was almost at the worn and rusty trailer housing the office where she was supposedly working that day. He took the last three steps, scraped the inch of mud off his ruined shoes and opened the trailer door. Wood paneling and the scent of three-day-old coffee greeted him. And silence.

The two desks in the main room were empty. No one stood in the cramped space. No sound came from the offices on each side of the trailer.

"Hello? Anybody here?"

The squeak of a desk chair moving across an uneven floor came from the room on the right. Then suddenly *she* stood in the doorway. He barely recognized her as the pulled-together executive from her headshot in the company's annual statement. This woman wore jeans, a plaid work shirt and a hard hat. But this was her. Charlotte Fillion.

"What do you want?"

She was one long, tall drink of water. Slender, with jeans that slid along her body like a second skin and blue eyes boring into him, she stood like a goddess.

His heart stopped, then bumped to life again. It had been so long since he'd been unexpectedly attracted to a woman that he'd almost forgotten what it felt like. Still, he dismissed the sensations oozing through him. He'd had the love of his life. Or so he'd thought. While he'd believed Mary Beth was supporting him through two tours in Afghanistan, she'd been cheating with his friend.

"I'm Jace MacDonald. I own Around the World Security. I've been sent here by the estate of Mark Hinton."

Charlotte Fillion actually laughed. "Huh. So, you finally found me."

She turned and walked back into her office.

Confused, Jace scrambled after her. "You know about the estate? You know Mark Hinton is your dad?"

"Of course, I do. My mother might have had to raise me alone, but she didn't make a secret of who my father was." She fell to the noisy desk chair, one that obviously needed a visit from an oil can. "We didn't go around announcing it to the world because the man was trouble. We didn't want any of that showing up at our door." She picked up a clipboard and began reading.

He inched his way to her desk. "The man wasn't trouble. He was rich."

She didn't lift her gaze from whatever she was reading on the clipboard. "You call it rich. I call it trouble. Bodyguards. Kidnapping attempts. Death threats. We wanted no part of that. Still don't."

"Well, brace yourself but you're in line to get a big chunk of his money."

"What would you say if I told you I don't give a damn?"

He gaped at her. Were all Mark Hinton's heirs going to be pains in the butt? Seriously. The first one they'd found, Leni Long, hadn't wanted her share of the money and now Charlotte Fillion was acting as if she wanted to bow out, too?

"I'd say you're crazy. But it's not my job to talk

to you about this. It's Danny Manelli's. He's the attorney for the estate. Whether you take the money or walk away, you have to sign papers."

"Fine." She held out her hand. "Give 'em to me."

"You can't sign them as an heir until you prove you are an heir."

"I'll tell my mom to send over my birth certificate."

In a lady's presence or not, he cursed, then told himself she was probably accustomed to it because she wasn't merely prickly; she also worked in construction where a man who hit his thumb with a hammer didn't say, "Oh, gracious me."

"We have your birth certificate. We need irrefutable proof. DNA."

"Want to swab my cheek?"

He shook his head. "Are you being rude deliberately?"

She set the clipboard on her desk with a thump. "I have eight weeks to get this building under roof. Eight weeks. Do you know what the weather is like in Western Pennsylvania in April? I'll tell you. It's unpredictable. So, I don't want to spend even ten minutes arguing with some fancy pants from the big city. I have work to do."

Jace couldn't help it. He laughed. When she got all fired up, she was like poetry in motion. Her forehead wrinkled, causing blue eyes flashing fire to narrow. The image implanted itself in his brain and he knew all he'd have to do would be think about it and he'd laugh again. And get that weird shot of attraction again, because the woman was like nobody he'd ever met.

But she was about to find out he wasn't like anybody she'd ever met, either.

"You're going to have to call in a replacement. Because come hell or high water I'm getting you to New York."

"Guess again, Ringo."

He frowned. "Ringo?"

"Ringo, Gringo, take your pick."

"You think I'm a greenhorn?" He chuckled and plopped down on the seat in front of her shabby desk. "Lady, I wrote the book on stubbornness, intimidation and getting my own way. You wanna have a contest? Give it your best shot."

"I can call the police, and have you arrested for trespassing."

"I invite you to do that, except then you'll have to explain to the police why you don't want to go to New York and accept billions of dollars from *your father's* estate."

She scowled.

"You think I didn't catch the fact that you've kept your biological dad's identity a secret?" He stood and leaned across the desk. "You think I didn't catch the fact that you know three million reporters will descend on this jobsite once I make it known that you're a Hinton heir?"

She glared at him.

"Oh, honey, that glare might intimidate guys who push dirt and hang drywall. But I did two tours in Afghanistan. I started my security firm right after I got home." His chest tightened when he remembered arriving home, remembered finding Mary Beth kissing Dave, remembered the two weeks of drinking himself into oblivion and then the day he picked himself up and started the company he'd always planned. "I've dealt with rock stars so high they didn't know their own names. Socialites who threw temper tantrums and billionaires' spoiled kids." He leaned in so close he could smell her scent. Not soft or floral, but pure female.

It jolted him that he noticed, but he had a purpose here. He refused to be distracted. "Give it your best shot."

Charlotte held the gaze of the absolutely gorgeous guy, and—damn it—the fierce expression on his handsome face made her swallow. His eyes were as dark as a moonless night. His black hair and the angles and planes of his face gave him a severe look, a countenance that probably scared lesser people. With a name like MacDonald, his ancestors undoubtedly wore that same expression when they fought with William Wallace for Scottish independence.

He meant what he'd said. But then again so had

she. She didn't get to this point in her career by backing down from what she wanted.

"Okay. So, you have ammo. You could out me to the press." Her instinct was to move in closer to show him she wasn't afraid of him. But she stifled that urge and leaned back. Casual. Composed. "But I have a job to do. I don't disappoint. I perform. Since we're at an impasse, let me suggest a compromise."

He retreated to his seat.

She smiled. Some days the way she could get people to do her bidding made her giddy. "Give me the time I need to get another foreman here."

"You don't have one on standby?"

She laughed, easing up, making him think they were friends. "There is no such thing as standby when a company is trying to make money. Some of our foremen get tapped for double duty."

"So, you gonna call one of them?"

"I told you. They're already doing double duty. I wouldn't be in the field if the company wasn't stretched to the max. We'll have to wait for one of my supervisors to get to a place in his project that he can pass off his current work to crew foremen and come here."

He scrubbed his hand across his handsome face and Charlotte took the opportunity to simply look at him. Black overcoat, with a white shirt beneath a black suit—probably silk—and a neutral-colored tie that was definitely silk.

A thought struck her, and she had to hold back a laugh. She'd bet her last buck he'd ruined a pair of Italian loafers in the mud.

"I can't wait forever."

She leaned back farther in her chair, appearing even more accommodating. "It'll just be a couple of days."

He sucked in a breath. "You do realize I have to guard you."

"Why?" She opened her hands. "Look around you. The only thing these guys care about is my ability to get them jobs, and enough money to support their kids."

"Doesn't matter. The official word from the estate is once we find an heir that heir gets a bodyguard."

"I don't need a bodyguard."

"It's not my rule. It's the attorney's rule. And it's warranted. We had a…misstep…with the first heir we found. She was on her own in a coffee shop and somebody took pictures of her, spied on her phone, figured out who she was."

The word *misstep* caught her attention, but her brain shimmied when he said *first heir.* She sat up on her seat. "I have a sibling?"

"You don't read the papers? It was all over the news when the reporter outed her."

"I work twelve-hour days. I don't have time for tabloids, magazines or even my local paper. I read three respected online sites. They don't print gossip and most certainly don't write about celebrities. They didn't even report it when my dad died. I found out from my mom."

He shook his head, but said, "You have two siblings. We've found you and your sister. She's the youngest heir, a twenty-six-year-old social worker."

Amazement flooded her. "I have a *sister*."

"Half sister. Leni Long." He paused for a second, then said, "Didn't you ever check to see if Mark had any other kids?"

She gaped at him. "How? Look at every birth record in every state to see if his name was on any birth certificates?"

"That's how the estate found you. Mark's name was on your birth certificate."

"No kidding. I already offered up my birth certificate but apparently only DNA testing will do."

"Hey, when there's an opportunity for irrefutable proof available and we've got scam artists coming up with some really great fake birth certificates, why not use it? DNA rules out the fakes."

"I'm not a fake."

"I know that and you know that, but we're holding everybody to the same standard."

"Fabulous." She sighed with disgust but peeked over at him. "Tell me more about my sister."

"She divides her time between New York with her boyfriend, Nick Kourakis, and her small town in Kansas where she's using a chunk of her share of the estate to spruce up the place."

"She's renovating an entire town?"

"Her hometown. She's probably the nicest person I've ever met."

The thought of having a sibling washed over her. Raised in the country, with only her mom, in a huge, four-bedroom farmhouse, she'd spent a lot of lonely hours. During the day, she'd wish for someone to toss a ball with or explore the woods behind the barn. Sometimes at night, she'd pretended she was on the bottom bed of bunk beds and her sister was above her. Sometimes that sister would be older and wiser. Sometimes she'd be younger and in need of Charlotte's counsel. But no matter how she'd imagined her sister they'd been best friends.

She and Leni Long had missed having a childhood together. But what would it be like to have an adult sister? What would it be like to have someone who shared her blood, her oddball past? Someone who understood being Mark Hinton's kid wasn't a joyride.

"Sorry. That just threw me for a loop, and I needed a second."

"You could fly to New York with me today and probably have dinner with her tonight."

The thought almost made her breathless and tempted her far too much. Especially when she had a job to do.

"We're still waiting for my replacement."

He slapped his hands on his knees. "All right. Fine. Then I'll set up shop here for a few days. Where you go, I go."

As he rose from his seat, the squeak of the main door opening rippled into her office.

"Hey, Charlotte?" Aaron Birmingham entered the trailer, calling her.

Charlotte yelled, "In here, Aaron."

The front-end-loader operator clamored across the common area and into her office. Seeing Jace, he winced. "Oh, hey! I'm sorry. I didn't realize you had someone from corporate in here."

"He's not from corporate. He's…" Oh, crap. The man was dressed too well to say he was a construction worker. And he was going to be following her around. She thought for a second, but there was only one kind of person who wouldn't look suspicious following her around. She smiled.

"He's my new assistant."

Aaron's face brightened. "So, you got corporate to loosen the purse strings!"

"A lot more than I thought I could," she said, pointing at Jace. "Look at that suit."

"Yeah, buddy. You really don't want to be wearing your good clothes here. Tomorrow you should come in jeans."

Charlotte leaned back in her chair and laughed. Maybe this wouldn't be so bad, after all?

Jace scowled at her, and feminine hormones

that she could usually control rose up like a tidal wave of need. She did not fault her hormones in the slightest. Jace MacDonald was tall, broad-shouldered, good-looking and every bit as cantankerous as she was. Any woman who liked a man who treated her as an equal would be attracted to him. The trick was not to let it show.

Unfortunately, she had days of him shadowing her everywhere she went. She'd have to hide the silly feelings at least eight hours a day. That was not going to be easy because he checked all the boxes of her list of things she wanted in a mate—

Her chest froze as another thought popped into her head. What if he was "The One"? He really did check all her boxes. Gorgeous. Tall. Strong. Treated her like an equal. And not intimidated by her.

Aaron snapped his fingers in front of her face. "Earth to Charlotte. I came in here to ask you about the area by the pond."

She came to attention quickly, not wanting her gorgeous bodyguard—

Oh, damn. He was her *bodyguard*—sent to her by her wealthy, uncaring, mean-spirited father's estate.

It wasn't an accident or glorious trick of fate that this handsome man had stumbled onto her jobsite. He worked for her dad—albeit via his estate. It would be a cold, frosty day in hell before she even considered getting chummy with one of her dad's employees.

She took another quick inventory of striking Jace MacDonald, dressed in black, looking dark and mysterious and so sexy even she could have swooned.

Too bad.

She dismissed her disappointment. Right now, she needed to get all the facts about his bodyguard duties for the next few days and come up with a plan to keep her distance, so she didn't slip up and do something foolish like flirt with him.

Because the last thing she wanted to do was get involved with someone, *anyone*, who had liked or respected the dad who had made the last twenty-eight years of her mom's life miserable.

CHAPTER TWO

JACE HEARD THE door close as Charlotte's front-end-loader operator exited the trailer. He waited two beats to make sure the kid was gone. Then he said, "I'm not your assistant."

"I couldn't think of any other way to explain you."

He sighed. He should be glad she hadn't blurted who he really was or who *she* was. Danny Manelli would kill him if another heir was exposed before they got her to New York where they could keep her hidden while they went over the details of the estate with her and waited for DNA results.

No matter how much he disliked it, Charlotte's explanation that he was her assistant was plausible. There was no sense arguing.

"All right. Fine."

She breathed a sigh of relief. She'd obviously been worried he wouldn't accept it, and, technically, his purpose in guarding her *was* to make her transition easier, not harder.

He backed off his temper a bit more.

Her gaze met his, her blue eyes wary. "I do have a couple of questions, though."

"Let's have them."

"What does a bodyguard do?"

"Generally, they protect you from getting killed, but in an instance like this my job is to keep the press away...and watch the people in your life to see if any one of them is just a tad too interested."

"Meaning?"

"Meaning I'll be scrutinizing the people around you to see if there are signs one of them has been approached by the press to spy on you."

She laughed. "That's ridiculous."

"Right now, I agree. No one knows who you are. The press doesn't realize they should be interested."

"So, you're pretty much just going to follow me around?"

"That and keep an eye on your people to make sure none of them is getting ideas."

"Where are you sleeping tonight?"

"Where are *you* sleeping tonight?"

"I have a house. A very safe house. I'm hoping you'll find a hotel."

He eased his hip on the desk, enjoying the odd shiver in her voice. She was so tall, so strong, so put together, that it was fun to unnerve her. "No such luck."

Emotion gathered on her face like a thundercloud. Fun or no fun, he'd gotten sufficient concessions out of her that teasing her was wrong. He knew firsthand what could happen if he got too friendly with a client. He had a job to do. Unlikely as it was that someone might have figured out she was a Hinton heir, he would do more than his due diligence.

"I'm not finding a hotel. I told you…where you go, I go. But I probably won't be sleeping as much as catnapping on the sofa nearest your front door."

Her face twisted as she thought that through, but her expression never reached acceptance.

"Come on. Cut me a break. The estate lawyer, Danny Manelli, is very particular. But I just have to be able to say I was in the same building as you."

"This Manelli guy calls the shots?"

"Yes. And he expects me to guard you. I don't have to be in your bedroom, watching you sleep. As long as no one gets suspicious about who you are, I can give you a fairly wide berth. But you have to let me do my job. Once your replacement is here, we can fly to New York, do the DNA and orient you to everything your dad owned, so that you'll be making an informed decision if you opt out of the estate. If you still decide you want no part of the money, then you're on your own again."

She groaned. "The things I haven't gone through because that man was my father."

"I get it. You can pick your friends, but you can't pick your relatives."

Her gaze leaped to his. "Your family is crap, too?"

He almost told her yes, just to give them something in common. But he didn't want to lie to her. He liked her no-nonsense way of dealing with things. He didn't want to lose that. He wanted her to continue being honest, so he had to be honest.

"No. My family's really cool. But I've worked for some rock stars who give 'crazy' a whole new meaning."

She laughed and tossed her pen to her desk. "Okay. It is only going to be a few days, then all this will be over. That man will finally be out of my hair."

Respect for her rose in him. She knew how to compartmentalize to get things done. "It's actually going to be more like two weeks. Your DNA sample will be sent to three labs. There'll be no mention of your name and though we'll put a rush on them all labs have different timetables. We might get one back in three days, another in a week and the third could take two weeks, but in that time you'll be briefed on everything your dad owned, including companies and investments. Even if you opt out, the estate wants to ensure you are making an informed decision."

She made a sound of disgust but said, "Okay." She sat forward on the squeaky chair. "I have work to do. And if we want to keep this charade true, your job is to answer the phone."

He squeezed his eyes shut but remembered his mission.

"Go sit at either of the two desks out there and wait for the phone to ring."

"While I watch who's coming in," he reminded.

"That, too." She grinned. "See? Look how convenient it is for you to pretend to be my assistant. There is only one way into this office and you'll be sitting in front of it."

He gave her points for that and headed to the door.

"Hey, wait, Jace... Mr. MacDonald... What do you want me to call you?"

"Jace is fine."

"Okay, Jace," she said, accenting his name in such a way that it sounded like a caress. Without the hard hat her pretty yellow hair fell to her shoulders in a nice wave. Her blue eyes sparkled.

He told his hormones to stop noticing her. He had a job to do. Nothing more. This wasn't an episode of *The Bachelor*. He'd made the mistake of getting romantically involved with a client once and only once. That ding to his reputation had not gone away easily. A wise man did not go down a bad road twice.

"The last temp we had left a bunch of magazines in one of the desks. Feel free to read them."

"Right." Like he'd spend an afternoon browsing

gossip magazines. He snorted and headed out the door to the first desk. The one closest to her office.

Because his Italian loafers were already ruined, Charlotte didn't hesitate to go onto the site. But she only went out twice. Jace really did look like someone from corporate following her around, taking in everything that was going on. Except a guy from corporate would be analyzing what she was doing, how she was spending shareholders' money. Jace looked for vulnerabilities. She could see it in the way his gaze faltered when it landed on a rip in the six-foot chain-link fence. His fierce dark eyes narrowed, and she made a mental note to send John Franklin out to mend it.

No sense arguing with a bear.

And he was a bear. Good Lord. She was an inch shy of six feet tall. She towered over most people. Yet, Jace had a good four inches on her. And muscles. When he'd taken off his overcoat and suit jacket, she'd seen his shoulders and chest stretching that perfect white silk shirt of his.

She'd bet he had flat abs, too.

She stopped the pitter-patter of her heart by reminding herself he didn't just work for the father she despised, but also gorgeous guys like him didn't go after tall, tomboy women. They went after cute, sweet, lovable types.

Too bad she'd already shown him her surly side.

She shook her head to clear it. Her goal wasn't

to wish for things that couldn't be. It was to forget about the possibility of anything between them. Considering that she'd just met the man that should be easy. She focused on the project—the slimy dirt, the pond that wasn't doing the job it was designed to do—and forgot all about being attracted to Jace MacDonald.

After their second trip outside, Jace scraped the mud off his shoes, shrugged out of his overcoat and took his place at the desk. She strode into her office and made the calls she'd been dreading. Before they'd gone out, she'd done a quick internet search on Waters, Waters and Montgomery and Danny Manelli. When that panned out, she'd called Danny to confirm Jace's story. When the estate lawyer parroted everything Jace had said, she knew this was real. She hadn't doubted it. She knew she was Mark Hinton's child. But she wasn't going to New York with a stranger without investigating.

Then she spent an hour looking at all the Kaiser and Barclay projects, evaluating the foremen, and made her choice. *She* was the vice president and director of operations for Kaiser and Barclay Development. She'd put herself in her current position at the jobsite because she didn't have anybody else to fill it. So, playing Rubik's cube with her foremen and projects, shifting and considering all the possibilities, she'd rearranged everything and found the best combination of people and jobs to get a replacement for herself.

"Good news, Skippy." After having made her calls, she breezed out of her office and into the main area where Jace looked like an adult sitting at a kid's desk. "I only have to finish out the week. Then we can go."

He rose. "Your boss found a replacement that quickly?"

"The director of operations is a genius," she said, motioning to him that she was ready to leave for the day.

He scowled. "*You're* the director of operations."

She laughed. "And I'm a genius."

She pointed at the door again. Jace rose and shrugged into his overcoat as she switched off the light. He walked out of the trailer in front of her, and she turned and locked the door before she led him to her big, black truck.

The sun had set long ago. The heavy equipment operators had already gone for the day. A lovely quiet had settled over the usually bustling ten acres surrounded by chain-link fence and smelling like spent diesel fuel.

He nodded once at the big truck. "Nice."

"Thanks. It was a birthday gift to myself."

He grunted. "You have good taste."

And here was another reason she usually ended up "friends" with the guys she found attractive. She loved engines. Loved speed. Loved power in a vehicle. Once she established that, men never saw her as feminine again.

But what the heck. Any minion of her dad's wasn't a potential match for her. Might as well pound a stake into the heart of her attraction to him and kill it once and for all. "What are you driving?"

He nudged his chin toward a huge SUV.

She sniffed. "Nothing says security detail like an enormous black SUV with tinted windows."

He ignored her sarcasm. "I'll follow you."

"Do you want the address in case I lose you?"

"I have the address."

His comment wasn't exactly matter-of-fact, but he wasn't angry as she expected him to be after almost six hours of just sitting, watching the trailer door and her office door. She supposed that was a bodyguard's primary duty. But the lack of movement or mental creativity would make her nuts.

She got in her truck and headed home, a mid-size, midcentury modern house. She hadn't merely designed it herself; she'd supervised every inch of the construction and decorated it.

She pulled her truck into the garage and Jace parked in her driveway. But she didn't enter through the combination mud room and laundry room as she usually would have. She walked out-side and guided him to the front door. No reason for him to see the two weeks' worth of dirty clothes she'd been avoiding.

As she punched the numbers on the security pad, he walked up behind her, then over to the front porch swing. Bending, he grabbed something and dragged it toward him.

Her breath caught. Had somebody figured out who she was and put a bomb under her swing?

He presented a duffel bag. "My staff had this delivered."

She put her hand on her chest. *Shoot.* She hadn't meant to act like a coward but all his talk of bodyguards and people coming after her had caused her brain to go in that direction. His fault. So, she would pretend it hadn't happened.

"Your staff is efficient. What's in there?"

"Work boots, work shirts, jeans." He shrugged. "A few notebooks and pens so I look like a real assistant, and my laptop so I can get some work done."

Impressed with his effectiveness, she smiled. "Wow."

"Oh, come on. I saw you with your staff. You say jump. They say how high. We're two peas in a pod."

She wasn't sure about being two peas in a pod, but every leader should have the ability to get his staff to do his bidding. So why did a stupid duffel bag under her front porch swing have her wanting to fan herself? She'd thought she'd killed the attraction.

So, he was competent?

Masterful.

Sort of sexy with the gruff way he made it all sound perfectly normal.

She told her brain to stop before it engaged other parts of her body, like making her breathless or stutter or—please, God, no—want to flirt.

Tossing her jacket and briefcase onto a convenient chair in the entryway, she said, "Bedrooms are back the hall to the right. Your room will be the first one. It has a private bathroom. I'm guessing you're going to want to change."

He grunted and headed down the corridor. The second his back was to her she squeezed her eyes shut.

Why did he have to be so gorgeous? And *tall*. For Pete's sake, men were rarely taller than she was. Yet, the first really tall, really good-looking guy she finds has to be one of her dad's minions.

If she didn't so desperately want to meet her sister, she'd be shipping Jace MacDonald back to where he came from. Not because she didn't like being attracted to him but because she couldn't have him.

She opened the fridge in her all-white kitchen with marble countertops and stainless-steel appliances, looking for something to make for dinner.

She absolutely refused to even be attracted to

anyone who worked for her dad. And Jace probably wouldn't want her, either. She'd been sassy and smart with him because when someone was on her turf, they had to accept that she was the boss. Besides, who was she kidding? Sassy was her middle name. She prided herself on being able to lead. She liked being strong and capable.

She sighed. Boy, now that she spelled that out for herself, she saw the flaw in her thinking. She'd always felt disadvantaged by her height but there was nothing she could do about that. Did she really need to be bossy, too?

She closed the fridge and headed for the pantry. She found macaroni and cheese, grabbed two boxes and returned to the fridge, this time looking in the freezer compartment and finding hamburger meat.

Perfect. She could brown that and stir it into the macaroni and cheese, then make a salad.

It didn't take long to brown meat. With prep work, it took about ten minutes to make the pasta, and she cut up the salad veggies while the macaroni cooked.

When Jace returned from his shower she turned to casually say, "I made dinner."

But her tongue stuck to the roof of her mouth. He looked pure Scot with his wet black hair, loose T-shirt skimming broad shoulders and a stomach that was as flat as the first cake she ever baked. Sweatpants hung low on his lean hips.

She worked to loosen her tongue and finally said, "I made macaroni."

Einstein she wasn't. But at least she'd stopped standing there like a fool, drooling over him.

"I see that." He lifted the lid on the pot. "I love this stuff."

"Me, too."

He returned the pot lid. "And the salad gives it a boost into a healthy meal."

"That was the plan."

He shook his head. "I don't remember the last time someone cooked for me."

Her heart melted. She wasn't domestic. She wasn't overly feminine. Everyone called her a tomboy. But there was something elemental in having a person appreciate her bare-bones domesticity.

She stifled a groan. She had to get her thoughts out of that place, or she'd have to worry about flirting again. "You don't have a mom?"

He chuckled. "Yes, I do. But my dad's family is still in Scotland. My older brother moved there two years ago to keep an eye on our grandmother. His wife is pregnant, so Mom flies over every other month."

She leaned against the stove. No mention of a wife and no ring. Still, she couldn't come right out and ask...could she?

No! For Pete's sake. This guy worked for her dad. Plus, everybody knew bodyguards weren't supposed to get involved with their clients. *She* was his client. If she made a pass at him, he'd rebuff her, and wouldn't that be embarrassing?

She turned and retrieved plates from the cupboard. "If you don't mind, silverware is in that drawer."

"Sure."

He pulled out forks and knives and grabbed a few paper napkins from the fussy carved marble container her mom had bought for her as a housewarming gift.

Working together, they easily set the table, then took their dishes to the stove to scoop out the macaroni.

When they were both seated at her round white kitchen table with aqua chairs, he forked a bite of the mac and cheese. "Mmm… Takes me back to grade school when my mother would bribe me with this stuff to get me to do my homework."

She laughed. "Mine used it as a reward for when I'd agree to wear a dress to a dance."

"Sweet."

"It was. My mother is the sweetest, kindest person on the face of the earth." An average-size woman, she hadn't known how to handle it when her baby girl was the tallest kid in kindergarten, elementary and middle school. Happily, the boys' hormones kicked in in high school and she was only the third tallest kid in her class.

"We were lucky to have good mothers."

She nodded. "It's probably why we're both so successful."

"That and hard work."

"Only someone who's struggled a bit to become successful says that."

He thought a minute. "I did struggle. I can guard anybody. It's getting clients—the marketing and PR ends of things—that I had to learn."

She leaned her elbow on the table and studied him. "But you learned."

"Learn or die."

She stifled a laugh. Damn it. She wanted to like this guy. She *did* like this guy. But not only was he her bodyguard—somebody who common sense said wasn't allowed to get too chummy with her—he'd seen her pushy, bossy side.

He wouldn't want her even if she wasn't a client.

They finished their meal. She retreated to her office to handle some of her regular tasks that had been sitting while she managed the new project. Jace said he'd scope out the place, then watch TV.

When she was done with her work, she took some pillows and blankets to him and left him in her living room. Most of the furniture in the house was ultramodern. Metal legs on furniture with simple, clean lines on glossy hardwood floors. But she'd found a way to fit a fat, comfortable gray sofa into that decor and was glad since she'd hate to have anybody sleeping on the thin cushions of a flat sofa while he guarded her front door.

Ten minutes later, she stepped into the shower, and the reality of Jace MacDonald shimmered through her. She was naked, water spritzing over her, and there was a strange man in her living room. Sure, she'd checked him out. She'd called Waters, Waters and Montgomery and talked to Danny Manelli. So Jace was legit.

But—

Holy crap. There was a man in her house. Not to fool around with, but to *guard* her. She thought about the reporters Jace had mentioned, then thought about her sister who'd been outed as an heir. Her mom had told her that her biological father didn't come around or even admit to her existence because he was afraid for her. She'd cited kidnapping threats and even death threats that led him to his decision to hide her in plain sight.

As a child, she hadn't thought too much of it, except that her "daddy" had been big and strong and smart so that had to be right. As a teen, she'd decided it was a cop-out. Though teenagers are usually overly dramatic, that assessment stuck because it was correct. What guy abandons a woman he supposedly loves, makes her raise a child alone—so far in the country she didn't have friends? A coward or a blowhard.

She'd chosen to believe he was both. And she could easily ignore his existence. Actually, ignoring his existence had made her life normal. Sure, she was raised by a single mom, but lots of kids had been. It nudged her to work harder to get her degree and make her place in the world, and she was proud of her accomplishments.

But now—

With a bodyguard in her living room and Mark Hinton's life finally intersecting with hers—

It all seemed surreal.

If she were smart, she'd focus on the gorgeous guy in her house, rather than why he was here, but then she'd have to deal with the damned attraction.

After one last check of her emails, she finally crawled into bed. When she closed her eyes, she realized she was going to have to tell her mom the estate had found her, and she'd be going to New York to prove she was an heir to the fortune of the man her mom had loved so much she'd never dated again. As if she hadn't grieved enough already when Mark Hinton died, this would make it so much more real for her mom.

She groaned. She'd never understood her mom's fixation with a guy who didn't want her, but, on the good side, she credited watching her mom waste her life with keeping Charlotte herself from making a fool of herself with men like Jace MacDonald.

Her mom's fixation on and pining for a man who didn't want her would keep her from even thinking about a guy who'd probably brush her off.

She settled on her pillow. She did not like being made a chump. Her biological dad had made suckers enough of both her and her mom. She'd held her head high, kept her nose clean and made something of herself. But that didn't mean that late at night, when no one was watching, she didn't feel the sting of being rejected. Her mom had adored Mark Hinton. He'd apparently also loved her mom. Things hadn't changed until Charlotte came into the picture.

She didn't think nonsensical things like her mom and Mark would have spent a happy life together if Penny hadn't gotten pregnant. She didn't blame herself for her mom losing Mark.

But she did know he hadn't wanted *her*.

Or her siblings apparently, if there were supposedly two more children, scattered around, none of whom had a clue they were an heir.

So that was on him.

But the feelings of being unwanted that she'd carried from grade school and almost the whole way through grad school had taught her that rejection was a powerful thing. It could mow down the smartest, fastest, most capable people. She'd been mowed down once, at age twelve, when she was old enough to put all the puzzle pieces of her mom's life together and realize *she* was the reason for her mom's bone-deep sadness. She wouldn't be mowed down again.

Her rationale in place, she nestled into her

pillow. Having survived the greatest rejection of all—a parent who hadn't wanted her, who'd changed his life to get away from her—not getting involved with the handsome Scot sleeping on her sofa should be a piece of cake.

CHAPTER THREE

THE NEXT MORNING Charlotte woke and swore she smelled bacon. Then she remembered she had a houseguest and she pulled the covers over her head. She was a Hinton heir. In some circles that apparently made her a celebrity. So, she had a bodyguard—a flipping bodyguard—who would be following her around the jobsite, while she tried to get oodles of work done before Western Pennsylvania's epic spring rains killed her chances.

She forced herself out of bed and into jeans and a plaid work shirt and headed for her kitchen.

Dressed in a T-shirt, butt-hugging jeans and sensible work boots, her heart-stopping bodyguard stood by the counter, drinking a cup of coffee.

She pushed her feminine happiness aside and said, "Good morning."

"Want some breakfast?"

"I'm not a breakfast eater."

"Strange for a woman who has bacon in her fridge."

"I like bacon on my cheeseburgers."

He nodded. "So, you're ready to go?"

"I normally put coffee in a take-out container before I leave."

He reached into the cabinet beside the coffee-maker, grabbed a mug with a lid, filled it and handed it to her. "Then let's go."

So that was it. Simple. No nonsense.

He pointed at the door. She headed for the one that connected to the mudroom and garage since he didn't need to follow her to get to his SUV.

"Where are you going?"

"My truck is in the garage."

"Unless there are tools or something you need in your truck, we take my vehicle."

"I have to ride with you?"

"You have to *everything* with me."

Too tired from a restless night to argue, she walked to his SUV, the crisp April air making her breath mist. He walked beside her, his head moving inconspicuously from side to side as his sharp eyes took in everything.

The craziness of it got to her. "My neighbors are going to think I had a sleepover."

He opened the door for her and peered at her over his sunglasses. "You did."

Damned if her heart didn't flutter. Still, she said, "Don't flatter yourself."

"Oh, I don't have to."

She climbed inside and he slowly closed the door. She didn't need to give him directions to the jobsite. He knew them as if he had memorized them. The second the SUV stopped, she jumped out, worried that he would open the door for her in front of her men.

Chuck Carter, a crew foreman, already walked toward her. "There's water."

"Well, of course there's water. It's April. You know. April showers and that whole thing."

"So, we keep going?"

She sighed. "No. Let me look at it."

Jace rounded the hood to stand beside them. Chuck glanced from Jace to Charlotte and back again. His eyebrows rose.

"Don't get excited, Zorro," she said to the almost-forty foreman. "We just happen to live near each other."

His eyebrows rose even higher. "An assistant can afford a house in your neighborhood?"

Jace calmly said, "I married well."

If Charlotte had been drinking coffee, she would have spit it across the hood of the SUV.

Chuck headed toward the heavy equipment and guys milling around. Jace walked behind him and in front of her. Not wanting Jace to arrive before her and look like the one calling the shots, she quickly maneuvered to the head of the line, taking control again. Leading the three of them into the field, she stewed a bit. Jace was probably a top-of-the-line bodyguard, but as an assistant, he was a bit pushy. And if he kept doing things like this, she was going to have to have a talk with him.

They looked at the water and traipsed around the site a bit before Charlotte studied the topographic map again. Jace glanced at his watch. Fifteen minutes. They'd walked, they'd yacked about dirt and now they were silently studying the map.

It was going to be a long day.

Finally, she made a decision, gave an order and they tromped into the trailer. As Charlotte talked on the phone in the back office, Jace washed the old, disgusting coffeepot and pulled a packet of coffee grinds from the briefcase he'd brought. He had a packet for morning and one for afternoon. He refused to die from whatever lingered in that old pot or drink the cheap crap the company provided.

The phone rang, breaking into the silence of the trailer. With a breath, he walked over, scooped up the receiver and said, "Kaiser and Barclay."

"Is this the Riverdale jobsite?"

Well, damn. Maybe that's how he was supposed to answer? All he knew was her company name.

No harm done, though. "Sorry. Only my second day on the job. I'll get it right next time. How can I help you?"

"I need to talk to Charlotte."

"Sure." He hit the hold button and walked back

to her door. "Pick up the blinking line. Some guy wants to talk to you."

"You didn't get a name?"

"You're lucky I didn't hang up on him. Your phone's an antiquated piece of junk."

"Because we're at a jobsite where new things can get ruined." She sighed, sat forward and punched the button on the ancient phone. "This is Charlotte." As the guy answered, her face lit; she leaned back on her chair comfortably.

"Hey, Jim!"

Jace's chest froze. Whoever Jim was, she clearly liked him. Maybe he was even a friend, not a co-worker. Not that Jace cared. He was only here to guard her.

She motioned for him to close the door, and though the muscles in his arms bunched and hardened, he casually reached in, grabbed the knob, shut the blasted thing and went back to making his coffee.

As it brewed, he found mugs and washed them, wincing at how scummy they were. How could they have dish soap beside a faucet and not make the astounding conclusion that they should wash their mugs? And how could she stay on the line for so long with a guy who was a friend, not a coworker?

Of course, he didn't know if Jim was a co-worker or a friend. He'd guessed from her gorgeous smile and the way her eyes lit that her caller was more of a friend than a coworker.

Finishing the last mug, he told himself to stop thinking about her—

Except what if the guy was more than a friend and she'd done something foolish like tell him about Mark Hinton...or, worse, made a date?

The strange something rippled through him again, tightening his muscles and making his stomach feel funny.

He swore his body was wrong. He was not jealous. He had learned his lesson about being attracted to or getting involved with clients with Misha. He would not do that again. But he did have a job to do.

Mugs draining on a paper towel, he ambled to the office, opened the door, walked in and sat on the chair in front of her desk.

She said a few things about Jim's house and a fix for his lawn tractor, then said, "Sorry. Gotta go. But we'll catch up soon. I promise."

She hung up the phone, then, shaking her head, she looked him in the eye. "What?"

"What you mean, what? You locked me out of a conversation that judging by the closed door was more personal than business. I gave you a few minutes, but I wasn't about to stay out while you made arrangements to have dinner with some guy."

"I would have let you watch. Isn't that what

bodyguards do? They go to a restaurant with their
client and sit at another table and watch."

He squirmed on his chair. She wasn't even pretending Jim wasn't a friend or hookup or something. "Yes."

"Okay, then we're good. If he calls back, I'll
suggest dinner."

Annoyed with himself and her, he rose. "No!
Damn it! You said we'd leave for New York at the
end of the workweek. That's tomorrow. We don't
have time to be squeezing in dates."

"It wouldn't be a date. He's married to my
friend." She toyed with a pencil, looked up and
smiled at him. "And just for fun, we could have
gone to dinner with them and pretended you were
my date."

The idea sizzled a bolt of electricity to the very
wrong place. He took a breath, squeezed his eyes
shut, prayed for strength, then popped them open
again. "If you want to have dinner with a friend,
pizza with the entire cast of a Broadway show or
go shopping for pineapple, I don't care. I'm trained
to guard you. But we have only one more day in
which the most important thing is keeping people
from realizing who you are. Keeping people from
realizing something is different in your life. The
more friends you see, the more people you talk to,
the more chance you're going to slip something.
Wouldn't it be easier to stay home with me?"

She sighed as if put upon. "I suppose."

"Don't 'I suppose' me. You get home at dark. You work another hour on your computer. Then you go to bed." He turned to the door. "You're just being difficult. You don't have time to socialize."

He was out the door before Charlotte could count to two. So, she stood and called, "That doesn't mean I don't want to."

She sat again, her heart stuttering and breath catching. She shouldn't goad him like that, but oh my goodness, he was glorious when he was mad.

She managed to behave herself the rest of the day. She even smiled and cordially offered to make dinner when they got home. But he insisted on cooking.

"You cooked last night."

"Macaroni."

"It was still cooking."

"All right. Fine. You can make dinner." Skepticism about his abilities had her wincing. But most single guys could cook. So, she stifled that. "I'll go change."

Kicking off her grimy boots in the mudroom, she stripped out of her socks, work shirt and jeans and slid into her most comfortable sweatpants and a T-shirt. Feeling human again and ready for food, she ambled out of the mudroom toward the kitchen. The scent of something sweet and meaty filled the air. Charlotte's mouth watered. If she were to guess she'd say Jace had found pork chops in her freezer, defrosted them in the microwave and was now grilling them in her oven...with barbecue sauce. Sweet, tangy barbecue sauce.

Suddenly her front door opened.

Standing by the oven, which had a clear line of sight to the door, Jace stiffened; his entire body went on red alert and he reached behind him to the waistband of his jeans.

Charlotte's heart stopped.

Then her mother entered, her mid-length yellow hair styled to perfection, a soft floral blouse over jeans and stylish boots.

Jumping in before Jace had a chance to pull a gun, Charlotte said, "Mom! What a surprise!" She gave Jace a pointed look and he relaxed. "What brings you here?"

Penny Fillion held out a square plastic container of cupcakes. "I baked today."

"Ooh...cupcakes!"

Penny ambled to the center island that divided the kitchen from the dining area. "It's fabulous to have a child who can eat and not gain weight. That way when I want a cupcake, I can bake them and not worry about eating the whole batch." She smiled at Jace, even as her sharp blue eyes clearly sized him up. "And you are?"

Jace said, "Charlotte's assistant," at the same time that Charlotte said, "My bodyguard. Dad's estate found me."

Jace's mouth fell open. "What the hell are you doing? What happened to the plan?"

"This is my mother. I don't lie to my mother."

Penny laughed. "She does, however, stretch the truth."

"It doesn't matter. No one is supposed to be told about the estate, so there'll be no slipups or surprises like someone talking to the press."

"My mom knows who I am. Why hide the fact that the estate found me?" She faced her mom. "And they want me to go to New York for a couple of weeks to prove I'm an heir so I can officially relinquish my share of the inheritance."

Penny sat at one of the stools in front of the island. "It's going to take you *weeks* to prove you're an heir? Why not just show them your birth certificate?"

Charlotte slid onto the seat beside her mom. "I offered it. They want irrefutable proof."

Penny sighed. "DNA."

Jace crossed his arms on his chest and leaned against a nearby counter. "It's more than that. The will has protocols Mark wanted followed so that the real heirs are vetted the same way the fakes are so no one can take issue with how it's all done."

Penny drew in a slow breath. "If nothing else, Mark was a planner."

Jace quietly said, "I'm sorry for your loss."

Charlotte peeked at him. Aside from Charlotte, he was the first and maybe the only person who'd acknowledged her mom's loss. It was the sweetest thing she'd seen anyone do in forever. This time when her heart swelled it was with appreciation, something warmer and sweeter than mere lust.

"Thank you," Penny said. "But life goes on." She faced Charlotte. "And I won't have you throwing away your future because you didn't like your dad."

"I'm not throwing away my future. I intend to run Kaiser and Barclay someday." She opened the cupcake container, ran her finger over the icing of the first cupcake, then licked it. "That's a future anybody can be proud of. Plus, it's all mine. I worked for it. Sacrificed for it. Got it on my own."

"Technically, you have to give your father credit for part of that. He did buy the farm and pay child support."

She gaped at her mom. "The man paid a fraction of what he'd have probably paid if he'd acknowledged me. And that farm was his idea to keep us hidden."

"Keep us *safe*."

"Potato, pa-tah-toe."

Penny looked at Jace. "I never win this argument."

Jace laughed. "I figured that out already."

"Don't let her walk away from a fortune."

"It's not my job to convince her. Only my job to protect her. Please don't tell anyone Charlotte's been found and she's being vetted as an heir. I know here in peaceful Pittsburgh it seems like second-rate news, but in New York, there are reporters who'd sell their souls for the names of any of the Hinton heirs."

Penny looked at Jace. "*Heirs?* How many kids are there?"

Jace quietly said, "Three. One older than Charlotte. One younger."

"Oh."

Charlotte's heart broke. She knew her mom liked to believe that Mark Hinton had pined for her as much as she'd pined for him. But the existence of a child *after* Charlotte was proof he'd moved on.

Jace broke the silence. "We haven't found the older one. But the younger one is Leni Long. A social worker from Kansas. Very nice woman. I know Charlotte's going to love her."

Penny perked up. "A sister! You have a sister."

Charlotte laughed. "Yes. I hope to meet her while I'm in New York. Even if I don't take my share of the money, I'd like to get to know her."

"Well, something good did come out of this, after all." She brightened and slid off her stool. "I smell dinner cooking and I didn't come here to intrude. Just to bring the cupcakes." She kissed Charlotte's cheek. "Let me know how it goes."

Charlotte said, "I will," and walked her mom to the door.

Penny grabbed the knob but stopped midtwist and leaned in to whisper, "He's adorable."

Charlotte rolled her eyes. "He's also my bodyguard and a minion of my father's."

"You've got to get over that."

"The fact that he's a bodyguard?"

"No. Hating your dad."

"I never really hated him. What I feel for him more than anything else is irrelevance. And though you might find that sad, it works for me to have put him in a tidy little box and not need him."

With a shake of her head, Penny left. Charlotte closed the door behind her and returned to the kitchen.

"I like your mom."

"Everyone does. She's cute and sweet."

She expected Jace to laugh or mention how different she and her mom were, but he didn't. He removed the pork chops from the oven, poured a noodle side dish of some kind into a serving bowl and took heated veggies from the microwave.

They ate dinner in silence. Charlotte's mind drifted as she thought about her mom, not quite sure if she should be worried about her. Having Mark die was one thing. Hearing he'd fathered a child after their relationship might have burst the bubble of hope her mom always held on to that she was Mark's one true love.

Still, she didn't say anything to Jace. He'd made

a nice comment about her mom and she appreci-
ated that, but he was her bodyguard, not her new
friend. No matter how often what she was thinking almost spilled out of her mouth, she'd catch
herself and pull back her words. Once she was
vetted, Jace would be out of her life. Stupid to
confide in someone who was part of a temporary
arrangement.

She said good night and slipped off to her bedroom after nine.

The next morning, having another person in
her house grew tiresome. She felt self-conscious
showering, but the reality of being Mark Hinton's
kid hit home in a way it couldn't when having Jace
MacDonald around was new. He'd now insinu-
ated himself into her work life, cooked for her,
met her mom and eaten one of the cupcakes her
mom had baked.

With the novelty of it seeping away, she realized this would be the rest of her life if she took
her share of the estate. With a bodyguard at her
side 24/7, she'd never be alone again.

She froze under the warm spray of water. She
liked being alone.

Except—

What if she kept Jace as her bodyguard?

The mere thought of having him in her life
more than temporarily kick-started her heart and
sent a weird kind of happy expectation shimmy-
ing through her—

She groaned. Was she daydreaming about a guy she couldn't have?

Charlotte Fillion did not do that!

She got out of the shower and dressed, getting more and more surly.

CHAPTER FOUR

JACE WOKE IN a good mood, glad they would leave for New York at the end of her shift. Watching Charlotte work the day before had made the tedious task of following her around far too interesting. The woman was so smart that Jace understood exactly why her crew was putty in her hands. If she gave them an order, it was the correct one. He almost hated taking her away from her job, but she had to be vetted as a Hinton heir. Then she had some choices to make.

But he'd also be back on his turf where he could control everything she did. His life would get easy again, the way it had been before Mark Hinton died—

Jace squeezed his eyes shut as a suspicion entered his brain. Mark's yacht had caught fire in the Caribbean. Though Mark put out a distress call and had a lifeboat, he wasn't there when help arrived, and they'd never found the lifeboat. After a thorough search, a significant lapse of time and a boatload of protocols and legal mumbo jumbo, he was declared dead.

Some mornings when Jace was still half-asleep, the thought tiptoed into his head that it all seemed so convenient, so coincidental. Mark's yacht catches fire. His lifeboat is lost…and Mark is free.

Angry with himself for thinking about something that couldn't possibly be true—real people didn't fake their deaths—Jace rolled himself to a sitting position on the sofa. Charlotte came out of her bedroom and his thoughts about Mark evaporated as his heart stopped.

She wore a light blue dress, fancy jewelry and high heels. Her pale hair framed her face with wide curls. The dress showed off her perfect figure.

He almost had to pound his chest to start his breathing again. "What's with the get-up?"

"You didn't think I would leave for New York for goodness knows how long without informing my boss, did you?"

He scrubbed his hand down his face. The voice coming out of the drop-dead gorgeous woman was Charlotte, but her fancy hair, makeup and high heels were throwing him. She was so damned feminine he couldn't stop staring at her, and that was trouble.

He had vowed—*vowed*—never to get involved

with another client and being this attracted to one put him on a slippery slope.

"I hadn't given much thought to your boss."

She slid a sparkly earring onto her earlobe. "I'm going to have to make up a plausible explanation for my absence while you shower."

He growled. "You're going to make me wear a suit, aren't you?"

"Damned if I know. I don't even know how to explain you since it will look odd that I'm traveling to New York for personal reasons with my 'work' assistant. I haven't thought far enough ahead to get to your clothes." She straightened her dress. "Go shower."

In the end, he wore the suit he'd worn on the first day, with the black overcoat and his work boots—since his loafers had been ruined. His pants fell past his ankles. Most of the boots were hidden and the rest he'd buffed clean. But with Charlotte beside him, he doubted anyone would notice his feet.

Neither of them spoke as they drove into Pittsburgh. Maneuvering his SUV into the parking garage, Jace automatically clicked into bodyguard mode, peering around at the typical concrete structure. Nothing unusual. Nothing to worry about. It would be a good, easy day.

Jace and Charlotte were the only two people in the elevator on the way up to the corporate office. Thick, awkward silence filled the space. It didn't bother Jace. It made him feel like things were the way they should be. Client and bodyguard. Not chatty friends. Not two attracted people. Bodyguard and *client*.

Charlotte sighed. "Your dinner last night was great."

He made a *"Pfft"* noise, as if cooking had been no big deal. He didn't want them to get close, but if she wanted to talk, he could do small talk. Ease her nerves. "Your mother's cupcakes were the showstopper. Besides, you cooked the day before."

"Yeah. Macaroni from a box." Still facing the elevator door, she gave him the side eye. "Seriously, you're a great cook. I haven't eaten a dinner so good in years."

"You know, with billions of dollars you could hire a chef who cooks like I do."

"Why don't I just hire you?"

He peered over at her. "You're thinking of taking the money?"

"No. But nice try."

"I wasn't trying to trick you into saying you wanted it. Actually, I understand why you don't." He sucked in a breath. If Mark had faked his death, this woman would hurt him. Thank God Jace really didn't believe he had. It was just a weird thought that popped into his head once in a while. He'd use his legendary discipline to even stop considering it. Because it was wrong. Pointless. Mark was dead.

"You're very good at what you do."

Surprise flitted across her pretty face, and for a second, he was caught by her beauty. High cheekbones, a strong chin, blue eyes that communicated everything she was thinking.

"Well, thank you, Jace."

The way she said his name almost had him sucking in another breath, but he stopped himself. Though her voice was like warm honey, he could not dwell on how that made him feel. Mostly because he knew she found him attractive, too. And that was trouble. Being attracted to clients wrecked careers.

He couldn't believe he had to remind himself of that. But everything she did hit him directly in the libido. He'd never been instantly, completely attracted to anyone before. Not even to Mary Beth. She was a beautiful brunette with a heart of gold, and he'd liked her before he'd loved her. Because that was how it was supposed to be. Feelings were supposed to increase over time. Not run over a guy like a freight train.

Of course, his relationship with Mary Beth had ended. Badly.

She'd broken his heart. Nearly destroyed his confidence. And the one time he'd seen her on the street, with his ex–best friend as her husband and an adorable baby girl… Well, he'd gone a little crazy, confided in a client, and they'd slept together. Years later, when Misha's dad disinherited her, she wrote a tell-all book to show her dad she could make her own money, and she'd told the whole blasted story. Except she'd embellished certain details. Details that made him look like a borderline stalker. Clients who'd trusted him suddenly looked at him differently. Clients with young wives or grown daughters fired him.

That's when Mark had taught him about PR and recruiting new business.

It's also when he'd vowed never get himself into that kind of position again.

Which sort of was his point. First, what he felt for Charlotte couldn't be anything more than hormones. Second, he had no intention of getting involved with a client again. Only an idiot made a business-killing mistake twice.

He was not an idiot. He would forget how Charlotte's simple thank-you had made him feel.

"I mean it. You're so good at what you do, no one ever questions you. Which means you have a good reputation."

"I do. I worked for it."

He sniffed a laugh. "I don't doubt that for one second. Which proves my point. You have what you need. There's no reason for you to take Mark's money."

"Exactly." She grinned. "I knew that a guy who

had successfully started his own company would eventually get it."

"Good God. Was that a compliment from you... to *me*?"

She glanced at her fancy watch. "I know you're more than muscles."

His ego loved that she'd noticed his muscles. Which was silly, but who could really understand the effect of hormones on an otherwise rational human being? Luckily, he really did have legendary discipline and he could also keep his ego in line.

The elevator chugged toward the top floor. One of her fancy earrings fell from her ear. He bent to pick it up and handed it to her.

Suddenly, they were face-to-face and close. He watched her eyes sharpen and her slow intake of air as if her breathing had stalled, even as his chest tightened and his mouth watered.

"Thanks."

Her voice shook the tiniest bit, but he couldn't find fault because his limbs felt clumsy and his brain had clouded. He had the slow burn feeling he loved. Not of risky passion, but leisurely, scrupulously thorough lovemaking—

Which was wrong. And certainly not something he'd let himself dwell on.

"You're welcome. Better check the clasp to make sure it's not broken."

She turned away from him and slid off the good

earring and slipped both in her purse just as the elevator pinged.

The door opened onto a busy reception area. A tall front desk stood as a barrier between the elevator and the company, but behind the receptionist were work hubs filled with people.

"Hey, April, how's it going?" Charlotte said.

The pretty redhead looked up. "Hey, Charlotte! Nice to have you here again."

"Well, I'm here but I'm not here. I have an appointment with Mr. Ferguson."

April punched a button on her phone. "Let me confirm." She spoke with the company president's assistant, then hit the button again. "You can go back."

When the receptionist pointedly looked at Jace, Charlotte easily said, "He's my assistant. New guy. I'm showing him around."

April nodded happily. "Good to see you finally got some help."

When they started down the hall, Jace said, "The whole company seems to know you didn't have an assistant."

"With computers I could handle most of my own admin. I especially like having control of my schedule."

Jace didn't doubt that for a second.

They walked through a door to an office in the back. "Good morning, Paul."

The young man in the small office in front of

the bigger one nodded once. "Good morning, Charlotte. Mr. Ferguson is ready to see you."

She said, "Thanks," as they breezed past and into the fancy office behind Paul's.

Jace's eyes widened. "Wow." The room was done with an Asian flare, complete with samurai swords and bamboo floors.

Charlotte leaned in a whispered, "I know. Reeks of money, doesn't it?"

He laughed.

A short balding man in an expensive suit entered the office from a side door. "Charlotte!" He walked over and hugged her. "And you must be the new assistant, Jace."

He shook Ferguson's hand. "That would be me."

Charlotte's boss studied him. "You look more like a truck driver."

Jace laughed, but Charlotte said, "That's because he's not really my assistant. He works for a law firm handling a legal thing for my family. Something confidential."

Though Jace wasn't sure where she was going with this, he remembered how she'd handled her mother and gave her some leeway. She hadn't said bodyguard. She hadn't said estate. And as she'd already hinted at that morning, a guy as smart as her boss would certainly question why she was going to New York for something personal with her work assistant.

Ferguson frowned, walked behind his desk and motioned for them to sit. "Sounds serious."

"It is, Brice. But it's also something that will literally be handled—totally over and done with—in two weeks. Unfortunately, it means I'm going to be in New York until it's resolved."

Again, she'd kept things vague. But also, honest. She might not be telling her boss everything, but she wasn't lying.

Brice studied her. "Are we going to be able to keep our projects moving without you?"

"I've trained my staff to work independently. Plus—" She held up her cell phone. "There's this. I'll take my laptop, of course, and be able to answer any questions, and video chat in on meetings, if need be. It'll be like I'm here in the office."

Brice bobbed his head as he thought all that through. "Okay. Sounds like you have it all worked out." He grinned. "Maybe this is our test of how well you've really trained your staff."

Charlotte laughed. "Bring it."

Jace just stared at her. The woman did not have a timid bone in her body. And if that wasn't the hottest thing he'd ever seen he didn't know what was.

He groaned. Damn it. This attraction wasn't going away.

And handling it was taking far too much of his brain power, brain power he needed to make sure she was safe.

* * *

Ten minutes later, they were out of the building, walking toward Jace's SUV.

Confusion nagged at Charlotte. She waited until they were seated in his vehicle before she said, "I thought for sure you would kick me or something when I explained why I'd be out of the office."

"You told him the truth."

"But no one's supposed to know."

He shrugged. "You didn't tell him the secret part."

"So, you didn't mind?"

"Hey, you had good reason for telling your mom last night and good reason to give your boss at least part of the truth today. What you said was perfect." He pulled out of the parking space and headed up the busy street before he peered over at her. "I like that you know how to be honest without selling the farm."

Those crazy happy hormones danced through her again. She found herself indulging in the pleasure of them and stopped them cold.

This was getting ridiculous.

She could accept that he was adorable and sexy. She could even let herself enjoy looking at him when he didn't notice. She could also respect that he was a successful businessman, a discreet bodyguard, a good actor.

But this thing they had where they clicked? It kept throwing her.

He cooked. She loved to eat.

She recognized his good points. He saw hers.

They were so attuned that she'd had to force herself not to talk to him about her mom at dinner the night before.

Damn it. Every day he felt more like "The One" but he couldn't be! She wasn't supposed to be thinking about him that way. And he absolutely was not thinking of her that way. But every once in a while he slipped, like this morning when she'd walked out of her bedroom in the dress with her hair fixed and high heels. His eyes had sharpened and for a few seconds he'd been speechless. Or in the elevator when he'd picked up her earring. They were suddenly so close he could have kissed her, and she swore he'd been thinking about it.

She told herself to get her mind off those things. They had two weeks together in New York. His turf. And she had to be a professional about this.

"Are we leaving this morning?"

"If all your business is done here, yes." Jace got on the interstate that would take them to her suburb. "How long will you need to pack?"

"I packed last night."

"Then I'll call the pilot. We can be in the air in two hours."

The pit of her stomach pinged. She wasn't afraid to fly but she did have a thing about takeoffs and landings. Just the word *pilot* gave her a queasy, awful reminder. Still, flying was the fastest way to New York and she always handled those few minutes of heart-stopping terror. "Sounds good."

"It'll be nice to get into a pair of real shoes again."

Forgetting all about her flying phobia, she laughed. In case she'd missed it in her list of his good points, Jace also had a sense of humor. A sense of humor that matched hers.

"I have to admit I was sort of impressed by how much you value honesty."

"No. I value my reputation. All it takes is being caught in one lie to ruin everything."

He made a sound of agreement. "I know how that goes. Almost killed my entire company by making one wrong move." He glanced over at her. "How'd *you* get to be so smart?"

"Grade school."

He sniffed. "What?"

"It's the height thing." She waved one hand above her head indicating how tall she was. "When you're close to being as big as the teacher in first grade, nobody even thinks to make you their friend. So, I learned to insinuate myself into small circles of kids playing games and went along with everything and pretty soon people stopped seeing me as a threat."

For a few seconds the inside of the car was silent, then he said, "I like your height."

Of course, he did. He was "The One." She just

knew it. But fate was ruining everything by having them meet when she was his client. He didn't even have to tell her it would be a conflict of interest to get involved with someone he was guarding. It was common sense.

Yet here they were…perfect for each other and not able to do a damned thing about it.

She wouldn't meet his gaze. "Yeah well, that's because you're four inches taller than I am."

He said, "Good point."

She stared out the window, thinking this through. *Come on, Charlotte. You are a renowned planner. A strategist. If this were a job, how would you handle it? How would you get rid of something that didn't work? Fix a behavior that was wrong, wrong, wrong?*

Jace suddenly said, "You know. I never put all this together, but Mark was my height. Being tall was one of his trademarks." He frowned. "People in Pittsburgh might not notice, but reporters in New York City, the ones assigned to flushing out the Hinton heirs, could see you with me and figure out who you are."

He thought for a couple more seconds. "I should assign someone else to you when we get to New York. Maybe even someone new."

She wished he would, if only to end all this confusion. That might even be the real reason he'd suggested it. To separate them. Not working together would render their attraction irrelevant.

"But Danny won't allow that. The Hinton estate is my biggest client. And we did have the slipup with Leni. He now insists I guard the heirs."

Charlotte sucked in a breath.

He peeked over. His smile gone. His face grim. "We're stuck together for at least two weeks."

And he didn't like it any more than she did because his reputation would suffer more than hers if they slipped up and did something foolish like kiss or, God forbid, sleep together.

Yet they were both tempted.

They reached her house and without a word she got out of the SUV. She headed for her room and grabbed her suitcase packed with enough clothes for two weeks. But as she fumed at fate, destiny or whatever force thought it was funny to have her ridiculously attracted to a guy she couldn't have, the oddest thought hit her.

What if this attraction was a paper tiger?

Sure. He was good-looking and intelligent, and they seemed to have a lot in common. But what if she kissed him and… Nothing?

She'd had this happen before. There was a guy she liked who went to the same coffee shop she did. He'd been cute and funny, and they went out on a date that was good. But when he kissed her… Nothing.

Nothing.

Despite all the signs, they hadn't had chemistry. She and Jace could be agonizing for nothing!

Jace MacDonald might kiss like a rock!

That was her salvation. The answer. A test to see if their chemistry was real.

All she had to do was kiss him.

CHAPTER FIVE

SOMETHING WAS GOING on with Charlotte.

Jace watched her sit in one of the brown leather seats of his jet and smile.

Again. All she'd done was give him an odd, goofy grin since they'd left her house.

"Those four chairs release, so they can be turned to form a conversation grouping."

Easing the back of her chair into a more comfortable position, Charlotte said, "Nice. This is a hundred times better than our corporate jet."

"It helps when you pay the extra money to customize."

She gave him the strangest look. Her eyes were bright. Her mouth had pulled into a big, fake smile. "Absolutely."

Okay. Something was definitely wrong for her to be this nervous. He didn't think she'd be jittery meeting the attorney for her dad's multibillion-dollar estate. She didn't want the money. Yet that was the only thing that had changed since he'd walked into her construction trailer. They'd boarded the plane that would take her to New York, where she'd jump feetfirst into squaring up her past.

Take the money or leave it; she was facing the biggest decision of her life. So, okay. Nerves happen.

Still, he could not present her to Danny Manelli when she was this jumpy. He was going to have to do something to get her back to normal.

"What do you say we play cards after we're at cruising altitude?"

"Look at you, talking all aeronautical."

"Cruising altitude is a common phrase."

"Right."

She settled back in her seat. He almost sat as far away from her as he could to give himself time to figure out how to get her back to normal before they met with the estate lawyer. But the oddest thing occurred to him.

"You're not afraid to fly, are you?"

"No! No! I'm fine."

He sat beside her. "Well, something's wrong."

"All right. Here's the truth. I'm not afraid of flying. It's the takeoffs and landings that give me the heebie-jeebies."

"Really?"

She glanced away. "Yes. I know it's an irrational fear, so I don't let it control my life. I fly all the time."

From the way she wouldn't look at him, he

sensed she was either embarrassed about something she would consider a weakness, or she wasn't telling him everything. Like maybe she threw up when the plane took off.

Whatever. He'd seen that hundreds of times with clients. "If you're going to puke, there's a bag in the seat in front of you."

"I don't throw up, you goof. I just—" She pulled in a breath. "Get a little high strung."

"A little? If your mouth pulls any tighter, you're going to burst a blood vessel."

She laughed.

"That's better."

The plane shifted, then started to taxi to the runway. Luckily, on this private airstrip, everything was close. They wouldn't spend thirty minutes with her nerves winding tighter and tighter as they waited for their turn. Their takeoff would be fewer than five minutes from now.

The pilot's voice came over the intercom system. "Good morning, Charlotte, Jace. It's a perfect day for flying. Our flight time is approximately ninety minutes. And we'll be in the air shortly."

"Shortly? What does that mean?"

"Did you want him to say we'll be taking off in exactly three minutes and forty-five seconds?"

"No. I just… Exact numbers make me feel in control."

Jace undid his seat belt, walked over to a cabinet and pulled out several magazines. "Here."

"What's this…? Is this payback because I told you to read magazines while you guarded the trailer door?"

"Nope. You need to amuse yourself. Shift your mind away from the takeoff, and before you know it, we'll be in the air and you said you're fine then."

"I am."

He nudged his head toward the magazine. "Then open that. Distract yourself."

She flipped the first page of the magazine. "You have some experience in this, don't you?"

"Yes. When I was barely more than a one-man operation, I did most of the traveling. Some of my clients had kids. Or they were elderly. Or they were high or drunk or both. I had to learn to deal with things."

The plane sped up, an indicator they were about to lift off.

Charlotte took a breath, flipped open the magazine and for the next three minutes read aloud about a family that was famous for being famous. "And at last rumors have been confirmed that Natasha is pregnant."

She set the magazine on her lap. "Well, good for her."

Jace laughed. The plane was in the air. Climbing, but in the air. Charlotte's nerves had clearly settled.

"All good now?"

"All good." She blew out a breath. "You do not know how much I hate being weak."

"Of course I do. I can't afford to be weak. If I'm weak at the wrong moment someone could be snatched or killed."

She leaned her elbow on the armrest and caught his gaze. "Really?"

She was a little close and the odd look was back in her eyes, even though they were in the air. "Truth be told, sometimes my job is more about having magazines, being able to get around a city and knowing how to cure a hangover."

"There's a cure for hangovers?"

"Hair of the dog."

"That's an old wives' tale."

"Not for everybody."

She pulled back, gripped the armrests with both hands and took a long, solid breath. "So, we have ninety minutes until I have the opportunity for another panic attack. What do you want to do?"

"I have cards. I have simple games." He released his seat belt and walked to another cabinet. "I like playing rummy."

"Me, too! My goodness, I used to play with my mom all the time, but I haven't played rummy in forever."

"Okay. Rummy, it is."

He got the cards and motioned for her to join him in an area in the back that had the same seats as the conversation area, except there was a table.

"Nice."

"I told you I have to be prepared for everything."

She sat as he dealt the cards. "It sounds like, in some ways, you're a babysitter."

"And usually for adults—who don't realize they need a keeper. I have to know when to butt in or when say, Do you want a magazine? Do you want to play cards? How about a drink? Or, Put down the whiskey bottle."

She considered that. "You're bossier than I am."

"I have to be."

She drew a card, added it to the seven cards she had and simultaneously discarded one as she set down her hand. "I'm out."

He gaped at her. "I didn't even get to play a card!"

She laughed with glee. "I know! I love this game."

It was her first spontaneous laugh since they'd left her house. His chest loosened with relief, which was normal when working to make a jumpy client calm. The happiness that surged was not. He squelched it. Her questions about his job had reinforced who he was and what he was supposed to be doing. No matter how talkative they got, it was still his job to protect her. Not like her. Not be curious about her. Not wonder what it would be like to kiss her, which was what had begun happening that morning. She looked pretty. Smelled better. And her honesty with her boss had made him want to grab her upper arms, yank her to him and kiss her.

Wrong on so many levels he couldn't even count them. He'd learned that lesson the hard way. But he was back to normal now and everything was fine.

They played cards until the pilot announced they would be landing in twenty minutes. Knowing the drill, Jace returned the cards to their box.

"Your choice. Stay here and buckle up or move back to the seats we were in."

"The seats we were in were lucky for our takeoff. I say let's not mess with a good thing."

He shook his head. "You're superstitious."

"No. I simply never abandon what works."

They returned to their seats and buckled in. The plane began its descent. Not a dive, but more of a layer by layer fall.

Until they hit the last layer. Then the nose pointed down and they headed for the runway.

Charlotte grabbed his hand. He turned his head to see what was going on with her. Her eyes were wide and bright with fear. He hadn't exactly forgotten her hatred of takeoffs and landings, but she'd been so calm—

"Distract yourself."

"With what! We put the magazines back in the drawer back there."

"Okay. How about this? Count to seven thousand."

"That won't help!"

"We have about thirty seconds till we're on the ground. Just do something that will occupy your mind for thirty short seconds."

"You want me to do something that will occupy my mind?"

"Yes."

"Totally occupy my mind?"

"Yes."

"Okay."

She leaned over and planted her lips on his.

The shock of it froze him. But when she eased her lips across his, tasting him, tempting him, his breath shivered and needs he'd been fighting all morning resurrected with the power of a tornado. He forgot all about diversions and conflict of interest and took command.

He took control of the kiss in a flash of heat that raced through Charlotte. The meeting of their mouths was heaven, so delicious she forgot she'd kissed him as a diversion.

Temptation rose. Urged her to take. She slid her hands to his biceps, letting her heart swoon at the strength of them before her fingers moved on, across broad shoulders to link at the back of his neck.

The fire inside her crackled. Despite her seat

belt, she shifted, getting closer, and sucked in a breath when their upper bodies met. Jace deepened the kiss. The fire roared.

Vaguely, in the distance, she heard a voice. With Jace's mouth on hers, their tongues twining and volcanic heat bursting through her, the thought of caring who spoke was laughable until she remembered they were on a plane. The plane had been landing.

They were probably on the ground and that voice had probably been the pilot announcing it.

She pulled back. So did Jace. Their eyes met and for ten seconds there was nothing but silence. That hadn't been an ordinary kiss. They both knew it.

It might have been the diversion she needed for the landing, but it hadn't helped her rationale about being attracted to him. He absolutely did not kiss like a rock, and he was every bit as attracted to her as she was to him.

Part of her thrilled at the prospect. But this attraction was not a good thing. They both knew that, too. They were where they'd started. Attracted and not allowed to be.

She fell back on humor. "And that, Skippy, is how you create a diversion."

She unbuckled her seat belt and started to rise, but he caught her hand and pulled her down again.

"We're both adults here. So, let's not play games. We're ridiculously attracted to each other, and we need to talk about this—" He motioned from himself to her. "Because it's wrong. You are a client. It is a conflict of interest for me to get involved with you. But more than that, it might impair my ability to do my job."

Disappointment flooded her, even though she already knew everything he said. Their meeting and being together was business. And not just for Jace. For her. She had a chance to get the dad who hadn't wanted her out of her life for good. If she didn't play this correctly, keep her focus, she could make some bad choices.

That woke her up.

She sucked in a breath, brought herself out of her disappointment and into her normal, intelligent state. Out there in the big, wide, wonderful world there was a guy for her. Someone as tall as Jace, as smart as Jace. Her equal. She would find him and not make a mistake by getting involved with someone who wasn't right for her.

"I get it," she said as the pilot left the cockpit and headed toward them. "And for your information, I knew all that. I was just checking to see if you kissed like a rock." She faced the pilot. "Hello, there. You did a wonderful job."

The handsome fiftyish pilot laughed. "It's not every day I get a compliment." He faced Jace. They talked about a few technical things as she maneuvered her way out of her seat to the compartment where she'd stashed her purse.

By the time she was ready to deplane, Jace was by her side.

They walked down the steps, then to a waiting limo.

When the door closed and the driver headed behind the wheel, Jace turned to her. "What the hell do you mean kissed like a rock?"

She picked imaginary lint off her navy-blue coat, so she didn't have to look at him. "Some guys can't kiss. I was hoping you were one of them and the attraction would fizzle."

"If I'd known that, I would have pretended to kiss like a rock to end this."

Her gaze jumped to his. "Oh, don't do that."

"Do what?"

"Ruin my memory of a wonderful kiss."

He grinned. "That good, huh?"

"Don't go thinking you're all that."

He just kept grinning.

All of Charlotte's competitive instincts rose. "You do not want to challenge me, or you won't like the results. Whether the attraction is pointless or not, we now know we're a good kissing combination. That's not going to make ignoring it easier. What we need to do is back away. Give each other a little space."

He grunted and shook his head. "That's what we were doing and doing well until you kissed me."

"Hey, you said divert my attention and I did."

She peered at him. "And I might have started the kiss, but you made it more than it needed to be."

"Maybe I wanted to see if *you* kissed like a rock."

She gaped at him. "You didn't even know what rock kissing was!"

He shrugged. "So, we use different phrasing for finding out if someone's a good kisser."

She sniffed. "I think you lost control."

"Really? Wanna try that again with me showing you what losing control looks like?"

Oh, Lord, yes. She would love to try that.

But that wasn't smart. So, she sighed and said, "No."

"Then don't press your luck."

CHAPTER SIX

As THEY HEADED to Danny's office, the limo got quiet. Charlotte wished she had that old magazine to get her mind off the thought of what it might be like to kiss Jace when he lost control. She didn't regret kissing him. That had been a necessary diversion, which nicely dovetailed into the test she'd wanted to make. But did he have to take it to the next level, tempting her to imagine what his best kiss would be like?

It didn't matter. The kiss had happened. The discussion after the kiss had fueled the fire of her imagination and she would deal with it. First, because he would. He could not get involved with her. His job depended on him being alert, sharp, and on his clients being able to trust him. She would respect that. But also, because she was on the cusp of getting her father out of her life for good. Distancing herself from him, his life, the worry, the threats, the bodyguards. It was her chance to keep the life she'd made for *herself*.

When they reached Danny's building, Jace

helped her out of the limo. Stepping onto the sidewalk, she glanced from side to side, taking in structures, people, traffic. "You know, Pittsburgh is bad, but this place is crowded."

"It's one of the biggest cities in the world."

"Thanks for the geography lesson."

He chuckled, back to being a congenial bodyguard. It boggled the mind that he had better discipline than she had, and she shook her head. No one had better self-control than she had. She *would* handle this.

He led her through the building's lobby to the private elevator in the back. They got in and in seconds the doors opened onto an office.

A tall, lean, dark-haired man rose from his seat behind a huge desk. Walking to them with his hand extended to shake hers, he said, "You must be heir number two."

"Yes. I'm Charlotte Fillion. And you're Danny Manelli." She gave him her brisk, professional handshake. "We spoke on the phone the day Jace arrived on my jobsite."

"You look like your dad."

Jace winced. "That might not have been the compliment you wanted it to be."

Motioning for them to take the seats in front of his desk, Danny said, "What am I missing?"

"Charlotte's like Leni. Not sure she wants Mark's money."

Danny groaned.

Charlotte sat up, went into business professional mode. She refused to look crazy for not wanting her part of the estate. "I'm a vice president in a development company. I don't need the money of a man who didn't want me, and I certainly don't want hundreds of reporters following me all day, every day."

Danny shifted on his tall-backed office chair. "Okay. I understand that. But you have anywhere from a week to two weeks in the city. First, we'll be awaiting DNA results, which will probably stagger in, considering we're using three different labs. But the will has also deemed it part of the process for you to view the slides of all your dad's properties, and to review his business holdings and private investments, so that if you do bow out, you will know what you're refusing. It's not my job to persuade you. The decision is yours. But the will insists on full disclosure to you of everything you're turning away. If you decide against participating in the estate, I will draw up papers and you will be out."

With that confirmation in place, she said, "Perfect."

Danny nodded. "Let me suggest, though, that you keep an open mind. Leni is doing a lot of good with her share. There might be something you want to do in your life."

"I'm doing it. I'm a vice president of a company,

looking to one day become president and eventually CEO. I have enough on my plate, thank you."

"Great. Then let's move on to the reason you're here." Danny buzzed his assistant, instructing her to bring in the lab tech. He swabbed Charlotte's cheek three times.

"We send three blind samples to three different labs. We put a rush on one, but not the other two. We don't want it to look like there is any collusion, so we use different labs every time. Without the rush on the second two samples, we get in line with every other sample that comes to the lab. So, it could take up to two weeks to get all the results. But we want all three for absolute proof. There's a hell of a lot of money here and people are coming out of the woodwork for a share. Even with our protocols, we know there will be lawsuits, but with our three-pronged DNA, blind sample-testing, the courts won't be able to argue if we have three people who match in all three tests and others who don't match at all."

Charlotte inclined her head. "Makes sense." She hated being away for weeks, but if this got her off the hook of Mark Hinton's hold, it would be worth it.

"In that time, you and I will have a few meetings about the estate, but primarily you'll be meeting with Nick Kourakis."

She straightened in her chair. "My half sister's boyfriend?"

"Yes. He has the slides that show everything your dad owned. Even if you bow out of the money end of things, you might want to take a beach house or the Jet Skis or one of his antique cars."

"Charlotte's more interested in meeting Leni."

Danny's face brightened. "Of course! That can absolutely be arranged."

"If you want, I can call Nick," Jace said, glancing at Charlotte. "We could have dinner tonight, if they're free."

Something inside her melted. She might not like her dad, but he'd given her a sister. That was the part of the estate she desperately wanted. "That would be great."

"Good," Danny said, rising from his seat. "I'll also let you be the one to set times with Nick for the days you can meet to see the slides of your father's properties."

Charlotte rose, too. "Days to see slides?"

Danny laughed. "Your dad owned *a lot* of things."

The thought that it would take so long to see everything her dad owned blew her away. "I know. But *days*?"

Danny batted a hand in dismissal. "We'll let Nick show you."

Charlotte was back to wearing the funny look that Jace didn't trust. The last time he couldn't read her expression she'd kissed him. The memory of it surged through him. Her soft mouth. The way they fit. The feelings that rose before he could stop them.

At the elevator, Danny shook her hand again. "It was a pleasure to meet you. Nick, Jace and I will do everything in our power to make your stay in New York interesting, so you aren't bored while you see the slides and get the rundown on everything the estate entails."

"I almost feel like I should go back home and let Nick send me the slides."

Danny shook his head. "No. We're working very hard to keep this from turning into a circus. We managed to do damage control after Leni's identity got out. So far, we haven't had a run of people claiming to be heirs. There are a few, but that number could double or triple if the estate gets too much attention."

"I'm putting up a building," Charlotte said with a laugh. "I'm not going to be making the circuit of late-night talk shows. My crew doesn't know who I am. I managed to sidestep the facts of why I'm in New York when I talked to my boss. My neighbors aren't interested in my comings and goings. I do not see how my returning home could be a problem."

"You act differently."

Danny and Charlotte turned to Jace.

Her face fell. "What? How?"

"When I first found you, you threatened to call the police on me. Now, we're having lunch and dinner like friends." He didn't mention that she also had a soft, sexy way of looking at him and had kissed him like a lover.

"That's because we're spending so much time together!" She rolled her eyes and faced Danny. "Sheesh! This guy. Noticing things that aren't there."

"I notice things people think they're hiding." That's why he could tell how affected she'd been by their kiss. She did a really good job of holding in her reaction. But he saw the facial cues, heard the softness in her voice.

"In any event," Danny said, interrupting them. "Go have a nice lunch. Jace is paying. He gets reimbursed by me. This time tomorrow, I will have credit cards and a bank card for you to use."

"Why?"

"It's part of the vetting process. Everyone with a legitimate claim as an heir gets a few hundred thousand dollars to spend in the two weeks they are in New York waiting for DNA results and being vetted by the estate."

Her eyes widened. "You're giving hundreds of thousands of dollars to the fakes, too?"

"Believe me, the estate doesn't miss the money. Plus, it looks good in the file that we treated you all equally, vetted Mark's real children the same way we did the group of 'potential' heirs. We're doing everything by the book."

After they'd said goodbye and the elevator doors had closed on them, Charlotte turned to Jace.

"He really does do everything by the book."

"Stickler for details," Jace said. But the elevator seemed small and she seemed awfully close. He'd felt her vulnerability in that meeting when they'd talked about her sister. Though she'd tried to be an executive with no feelings, her emotions were right there for anyone who knew what to look for. He chalked it up to her desire to meet Leni, but he'd still pay close attention. Look for shifts. Indicators that she might decide the whole process was nonsense and bolt—

Or that she might kiss him again.

God only knew what was going on in that supersmart, superanalytical brain of hers and he was going to have to manage it for two long weeks.

They got into the limo and headed for a quiet, exclusive restaurant, where the people who saw them wouldn't care if she was a Hinton heir or a member of a royal family because they themselves were heirs and heiresses, princesses, kings and billionaires.

After they ordered, she stayed quiet. He had a million topics he knew she'd respond to, but that was the problem. They were so compatible. Add that to their attraction and they were prime candidates for a misstep. All he had to do was think about that kiss and his brain shifted from work to molten need. He no longer saw her as a client and thoughts of her being his lover teased him. And that was how mistakes were made. The Hinton estate was huge, and he was responsible for her. He couldn't afford any slipups. He didn't want her found out, preyed upon, hurt.

He said the one thing he was sure would keep them on the right track and take her attention where it needed to be. "As soon as we get settled, I'll call Nick and set up dinner tonight, if he and Leni are available."

He knew that was the draw for her. The reason she hadn't just kicked him out of her office that day at her jobsite trailer and let the estate do her bidding. She wanted to meet Leni. Jace would introduce her to Leni, make her happy and keep her happy for the two weeks she was his responsibility.

After that…

He had no idea. She seemed to think she could walk away from the money and all would be well. But it wouldn't. She could run but she could never hide, and if she thought refusing the money would make her less interesting to reporters, she was sadly mistaken. The way Jace saw this, that would actually make her more interesting to reporters and curiosity seekers.

There was no walking away from this for her. He simply didn't want to be the one to tell her.

After lunch, his limo took them to the Upper East Side and his condo. The driver came around and opened the door, but Jace helped Charlotte out. She emerged from the car, a picture-perfect blonde in her pale blue dress, with a navy-blue coat over it, and sunglasses, looking Princess Kate beautiful and Jackie Kennedy elegant.

Which made him very glad he'd decided to keep her at his condo rather than a hotel. She was too tall and too pretty. Any arbitrary photographer could look at her, assume she was a model and snap a picture. Months later, after the estate announced the heirs, that photo would be worth a small fortune.

He squeezed his eyes shut. Damn. He was going to have to tell her that she couldn't hide from this by refusing her share. A woman could not look like Charlotte did without attracting attention. Bow out of the estate or not, she would become a curiosity to reporters and an easy mark to kidnappers because she wouldn't have the protection the other heirs had.

As the driver walked to the trunk for their suitcases, they turned to enter the sand-colored stucco building and she said, "This isn't a hotel."

"It's my condo building."

One of her eyebrows rose above her black sunglasses. "You think this is wise?"

The glass doors automatically opened, granting them entrance into the quiet lobby. The doorman, the only person in the room, saluted Jace, and he nodded once as he led Charlotte to the elevator. He pressed the button for his floor, then ran his key fob over the private security panel. His condo might be luxurious, but it wasn't the only one on the floor, so they couldn't completely lock the floor.

As the elevator zoomed upward, he asked, "Do I think what is wise?"

She turned her head. He couldn't see her eyes behind the big, black glasses. "Us staying in the same condo."

He knew what she meant. But she didn't have to worry about him or their attraction. Now that he'd figure out just how much trouble she could be in if she refused the money, there'd be no more friendly talks. No chances for them to realize how alike they were or how much they enjoyed each other's company.

"It's the safest way to do this. Besides, even if you were staying in a hotel, I'd be in the sitting room of the suite, catnapping on the sofa, watching the door."

She sighed.

He shook his head. "Come on. In those sunglasses you look like a supermodel. Some photographer scrounging for celebrities could see you and snap a picture knowing he could figure out who you were later. Then when the news broke about you being a Hinton heir, that photo could be all over the city."

The elevator doors opened. "This city must be desperate for entertainment."

He walked her to his condo door. "This city is odd. We have everybody here from Broadway stars and financial gurus to maids and garbage-men. Every man wants to be the guy who finds himself in an elevator with Jennifer Lopez and every woman wants to be the one who's suddenly standing next to a prince on the sidewalk."

She pondered that for a second. "That prince's bodyguards would be fired for letting someone get that close."

"True, but not my point." He opened the door onto the foyer of his condo. "My point is in those sunglasses you look like somebody. Better to have you here, where no one will get curious enough to take your picture." He held back a wince real-izing this was his opportunity to give her the bad news about refusing her dad's money. He couldn't jump in with both feet, but this was as close of a segue as he was going to get. "And once the es-tate papers are filed and everybody knows you are one of Mark Hinton's kids, one of his *heirs*, if you accept the money or not that picture could be used to find you."

"I suppose." She shrugged out of her coat.

"You suppose? Do you realize how much potential danger you're in?"

She laughed. "Look at me. I'm not easy prey. Plus, I won't have any money. Reporters might find it fascinating that I refused billions of dollars, but that will fizzle in a few years when they see how boring I am. And kidnappers? Why take a normal woman?"

"Because you might not have billions, but your biological family will. A kidnapper won't call your mom. They'll call Leni...or your other sibling once we find him or her. You'll be an easy target. Which will make Leni and your other sibling's life more difficult."

"Damn." She took a breath. "You make a good case."

"Because I'm correct."

"Maybe. I'll need to think about it."

Shaking his head, he led her into the open-floor-plan living room, dining room and kitchen. Such a stubborn woman. He certainly hoped the result of her thinking was the realization that she couldn't simply walk away.

"Nice digs."

"Thanks." He glanced around at the white kitchen with stunning shiny white tile floors and black quartz countertops. "I did none of it myself."

Beyond the kitchen he had a blue love seat flanked by white chairs with a blue, beige and gray area rug. But the lure of the space was just beyond the dining room table with its four navy-blue wingback chairs. A floor-to-ceiling window curved from one side of the room to the other, displaying a breathtaking panoramic view of the Upper East Side.

After stashing her sunglasses in her purse, which she tossed on one of the chairs, she walked to the blue love seat. "Bet you don't sleep here on restless nights."

He snorted. "No."

She glanced at him. "Why so small? Why not a sofa?"

"Nobody really ever sits there. The whole living room is just for show." He motioned her to the right. "Come here."

He opened the door on what should have been a bedroom but which he'd converted into a space with a pool table and a big-screen TV.

"Now that's what I'm talking about." She faced him. "You're either into football, baseball or hockey."

"A man can watch basketball on a big screen, too."

"Agreed." She walked in reverently. "My next project is to put a room like this in my basement."

One short conversation and they were two peas in a pod again. If they could pursue this, they wouldn't merely be lovers; they'd be friends. A relationship with her would be easy, natural.

Which was the totally wrong direction for his thoughts. Forcing his brain out of that spot, he took the conversation away from how they both liked sports and comfortable rooms, and to a neutral place. "With a one-story house, your basement is probably huge."

"It is. I could hold wedding receptions and bar mitzvahs down there."

"A nice side income."

"Yeah, in another century I'd have as much money as my supposedly wealthy dad had."

He snorted. "Or you could just take your share of the estate."

"More fun to earn it on my own."

He couldn't argue that, which almost annoyed him. Why did she have to be so smart, so fun? He could imagine what making love to her would be like. She'd be involved, probably throw her whole self into it.

Picturing it, he held back a groan and led her out of the TV room. "I wanted you to see you'll be comfortable here for two weeks."

"What will you be doing?"

"Guarding you. But I also have a business to run." He guided her a little farther down the hall. "This is bedroom number three of four. Bedroom one—" he pointed beyond the open-floor-plan living area to the other side of his condo "—is a maid's quarters." He pointed a few feet in front of them. "That's the master bedroom." He grabbed the doorknob to the room beside them. "And this is where you'll be staying."

The white distressed wood bed sat on a bright yellow print rug. Yellow curtains blocked out the sun. For the first time since he'd had this place decorated, he actually noticed it. But that was because it suited her. Bright and sunny. Happy. Easy on the eyes.

Getting even more annoyed with himself, he forced his mind back to what he was supposed to be doing and motioned to a closed door. "There's a bathroom and a closet behind that. You'll be perfectly comfortable."

She caught his gaze. "Will I?"

He knew she wasn't talking about the pillows or the proximity to the bathroom. Memories of their kiss collided with all the other images he'd unwittingly been conjuring, and his hormones awoke and battled to take charge. He imagined she had the same problem and had to inhale a breath to squelch the bright light that snapped on in his ego. Though it was totally wrong, he loved that she was attracted to him.

He stomped out the images, killing the bright light of his ego. "Yes. I'm a professional."

"So you've said."

He didn't remember how they got to be standing so close. If she'd taken a step or if he'd taken a step. But they were near enough to touch without stretching, close enough to kiss again.

Warmth flooded him along with the urge to grab her, kiss her and do all the things he knew they could do together. He stared into her eyes, hoping she'd give him a look that would make him think he was imagining the attraction was mutual, but all he saw was curiosity. Would they be as hot together as their kiss hinted they would be?

If he'd known she'd been checking to see if he kissed like a rock, he could have shut this whole attraction down with one awkward, sloppy kiss. But his inner guy laughed at him. She'd taken him by surprise, lured him to wrestle for control... Did he really think he could have shut that down?

He stepped back, wanting to shake himself silly. One taste of her had upped the temptation. And that's what killed him. Usually when he made a firm decision about anything, he was like a rock of determination.

He called on that discipline to ignore everything but his need to keep her hidden while she was in New York. "Yes. I know you're safe with me. You're a stubborn woman who I believe has made up her mind to do the right thing about our attraction."

She laughed. "Calling on my innate stubbornness to keep me in line so that all you have to worry about is yourself? That's good."

"What can I say? I've had a bit of experience in this."

Her eyes widened "You've kissed other clients?"

He cleared his throat. "Once. But I've had better reasons to learn how to keep my charges in line. Experience is experience. Some things translate."

She sniffed a laugh.

Feeling like he'd dodged a bullet when she didn't ask him to elaborate about the client he'd kissed, he said, "This is the perfect time for you to set up your laptop and check in with your job-sites. I'm going to call Nick and see if he and Leni have plans for tonight. After that, how about a few games of pool?"

"I'm not sure how long I'll be on the phone with my foremen."

Even as she said that, the doorman appeared with her luggage, including the briefcase Jace assumed held her work.

"That's fine." It would make his life a hundred percent easier if she could entertain herself until it was time to go to Nick and Leni's. "I'll let you know what Nick says about dinner tonight."

He closed the door as he left. But before walking down the hall, he stopped and sucked in a breath. For the first time since his wife cheated, he genuinely clicked with a woman. The sexual attraction was off the charts, but what he felt wasn't just lust. Charlotte was smart, interesting, funny.

And he had to walk away.

If the Hinton estate wasn't his biggest client, he would seriously consider bowing out because he truly liked her. But the Hinton estate was his best customer and he had twenty employees with kids to feed on that job alone. He couldn't lose all that for someone he'd known a couple of days.

But oh, it would be so much easier if he could give in to the temptation of her pretty eyes, luxurious hair and smoking-hot body—

Or would it?

Charlotte was a nice woman. Smart, articulate, sometimes even cutely sassy. But deep down she was good. And he'd been hurt enough to have walls the size of China around his heart. He might like her, but he'd never love her. He'd never trust his heart like that again.

And, at some point, she'd realize that and be hurt.

Did he really want to hurt Charlotte?

No. He wanted to protect her. Even from himself.

CHAPTER SEVEN

CHARLOTTE TURNED TO unpack her suitcase, but her insides quaked. That was the sexiest, non-flirty conversation she'd ever had with a man. They might have talked about not doing anything about their attraction, but the desire in his eyes told a whole different story and that clicked with something in her. It was everything she could do not to kiss him again.

It wasn't like her. She always had her stuff together. If she needed to be disciplined, she could be a rock.

Yet, no matter how hard she tried, she couldn't pull that rabbit out of her hat when she was around Jace. She'd even forgotten she hadn't checked in with her crew. Jace had had to remind her.

With a shake of her head, she set up her laptop on a small table by the window. Determined to get her mind off Jace, she busied herself with pulling up budgets, estimate sheets, labor allotments, and began calling her foremen for progress reports.

Midway through her second conversation, he

appeared at her door. "Dinner tonight at Nick's penthouse. I'm not risking you and Leni out in public together."

"Just a sec, Pete," she told her foreman before she put him on hold and glanced over at Jace. "Really? We're sneaking around?" This was the one thing that could get her mind off how sexy he was. The estate's insistence that she have a bodyguard. It was overkill. Plus, take away the bodyguard, take away the attraction. Undoubtedly, Jace thought he was clever overguarding her and Leni to make his point about heirs being targets—but she didn't buy it. She hadn't bought it when Mark Hinton had said she was in danger simply by virtue of being his daughter and she didn't buy it now.

"Why don't you just change my name to Double-O-Seven?"

"Because you're not a spy. You're merely being careful for the next two weeks."

"I thought you said I'd have to be careful forever."

"If you refuse your share once DNA proves you're an heir, you won't be my problem anymore."

That simultaneously relieved her and squeezed her heart. He'd been in her life 24/7 for only three days, but it was impossible to wrap her head around never seeing him again.

She groaned internally.

Where was her legendary discipline? She'd dated at least twenty guys and had never once been dumped. She'd always seen trouble before they did, and no matter how attractive the guy, she could walk away. Around Jace she forgot all that.

He grinned. "But dinner at their penthouse also means we can wear jeans."

She couldn't let him see that just the thought of not having him in her life threw her, so she smiled as if absolutely thrilled about getting to wear jeans. "That is a plus."

"Good. I'll tell them we'll be there."

He left and she tossed her hands, annoyed with herself. Especially since she had work to do.

She took Pete off hold and settled in to hear reports and help problem solve to forget about Jace and her fire-breathing monster of an attraction.

At five-thirty she headed for the shower to get ready for dinner with her sister.

Her sister.

The other thing that could make her forget about sexy Jace.

Having a sister seemed surreal. Even the normal tasks of drying her hair, sliding into jeans and a sweater, pulling her leather jacket out of her suitcase, felt different, weightier somehow.

She wasn't an only child. Even if she decided not to participate in the estate, she and Leni Long would always be sisters.

And there was another heir. Another sister,

maybe. Or perhaps a brother? She might have a *brother.*

What would that be like?

She didn't even try to make conversation in the car. Neither did Jace. Now that they weren't dancing around the attraction, he was only her bodyguard. Barely talking to her. Watching out the car window. Because she was an heiress.

Not merely a woman with a sister and a possible second sister or brother. But a woman connected to billions of dollars.

Damned if that didn't make it hard to breathe.

That's what Jace had been trying to tell her. She could bow out, but she'd always be linked to the Hintons, the money, the notoriety. A sister she didn't know, another sibling who hadn't yet been found.

What if they didn't like each other?

What if one of them was a criminal? A drug addict? A con artist?

She faced Jace. "You are coming in for dinner, right?"

Jace snorted. "Nick is a good friend of mine. Even if you weren't here, he and Leni would feed me."

"I'm just saying I'd feel weird if you sat in the car and waited for us."

"And it would also be nice to have a buffer."

She held back a sigh. Damn him and his perceptiveness. "Yes. If things get awkward between me and Leni, like if we can't think of anything to talk about, feel free to jump in with interesting conversation topics." She shook her head. "You have no idea how freaky this is. I spent my entire life as an only child. Now I'm part of a tribe."

Jace slid a glance her way. "The great Charlotte Fillion is nervous?"

"Kind of nervous but more amazed. I've wanted a sister forever."

The limo stopped. Jace got out and offered his hand to help her out. "Good. You should be amazed. I told you. Leni is a wonderful person. You are going to love her."

They walked into a building so elegant that Charlotte looked around in awe.

After Jace asked the doorman to inform their hosts that they were on their way up, she said, "I'd love to see the blueprints for this."

Leading her to a private elevator, Jace laughed. "Always working."

"Nope. Still stuck on amazed." Not to mention confused, awestruck and overwhelmed.

He punched some numbers into a keypad; the elevator door opened, and they stepped inside.

"Wow."

"Nick's family had money but when Nick took over their business it blew up. I can't even imagine their net worth now. He has a knack for finding the right investment at the right time."

"In other words, he's as wealthy as my sister."

"It makes them a good match."

She nodded. "No worry that he's dating her for her inheritance. No fights about money."

He inclined his head to the right, studying her. "You do know that you're moving into a whole new social circle, right?"

She swiped her hand down the sleeve of her jacket, pretending to brush off dust. "I'm not moving anywhere."

"Maybe not, but every time you visit your sister, you'll be stepping into that world whether you want to or not."

She'd figured that out in the car. But that didn't mean she wouldn't seek a workaround. "We can always meet for lunch at a diner on the interstate halfway between Pittsburgh and New York."

"And she'll be bringing bodyguards."

"Who will sit at the next table." She shook her head. No matter how hard this pressed in on her, she couldn't let Jace know how confused she was, how a simple refusal of the Hinton fortune had become complicated. Their being able to talk, being so attuned to one another, was part of the attraction, and right now she was annoyed with the attraction. Annoyed with herself for having so much trouble fighting it when Jace had made it clear he wasn't interested.

"Sheesh. I thought we'd talked about this. I'm fine."

The elevator door opened onto a huge open-floor-plan space with a kitchen and seating area with pool table and bar by the wall of windows.

"Wow."

A petite brunette in jeans and a peach-colored sweater and a tall dark-haired man walked over to meet them. "Charlotte?"

"Leni?"

"Yes!" The smaller woman hugged her. "And this is Nick."

As she stepped back, Charlotte said, "You're so small!"

Leni laughed "You're so tall!"

Both Jace and Nick said, "Mark was tall."

Leni laughed again, but Charlotte gave Jace the side eye. There was something about the way they'd said that simultaneously that gave Charlotte an odd feeling.

Leni motioned to the seating area. "Come in! Janine is making her famous beef tenderloin with shallots." She gasped. "Oh, shoot! I never thought to ask if you were a vegetarian or vegan."

"Nope. We're good," Charlotte said, staring at Leni, studying her. "I'm so amazed to have a sister."

Leni caught her hand and squeezed. "Me, too. I was an adopted only child. I was lucky, though. My parents are wonderful. I can't wait for you to meet them."

Charlotte followed Leni to an aqua sofa. "My mom's pretty cool, too."

As Leni sat, she said, "I can't wait to meet her."

"I'm sure she'll love you." Charlotte glanced around. "So, you're a social worker?"

"I trained to be. But once I sorted through everything, I saw I could put my life to better use with philanthropic work." She smiled. "And you're a vice president in a development company?"

"Yes." Clearly Leni had done her homework. "I'm angling to become president of Kaiser and Barclay, then CEO, then chairman of the board."

Leni frowned. "You're staying at your job?"

"Of course. I've been working toward this for years. College, grad school, four years of slogging through jobsites—"

"In four years, you became a vice president?"

Nick said, "Impressive."

Jace laughed. "I watched her work. She's a dynamo."

Nick rose from the sofa. "Can I get anyone a drink? Wine, maybe?"

Charlotte said, "A glass of wine would be great. Whatever you recommend. I'm not picky." And she was also desperate for something to soothe her nerves. She liked Leni. It was hard not to like an adorable pixie. But her soul had swelled with pride when Jace said she was a dynamo. He understood her in a way no one in her life ever had. That's why she could be herself with him.

That's why she liked him. Why this attraction had latched on and wouldn't let go. Since the day she'd met him, she'd been only herself. And he still liked her—even though he wasn't supposed to. He'd all but admitted he was fighting the attraction, too. Though with much more success than she was.

"Anyway," Leni said. "I can't wait to hear everything about your childhood. I'm so happy to have a sister."

"I'm happy to have a sister, too," Charlotte said. "I'm not sure if I had an odd upbringing or a good one. My mom and I lived on a farm about five miles outside a little town near Pittsburgh. Though I had a vegetable garden, we didn't work the land. We leased it to a neighbor who even used our barn to store hay. So that was fun."

"You lived in the country! I grew up in a small town. My dad was a construction worker. My mom worked in the diner. When I turned sixteen, I waitressed there, too, to save money for university tuition."

"I was a salesclerk." Charlotte laughed. "That's how I saved for tuition."

Nick brought the wine. Charlotte accepted her glass with a smile. "Danny tells me you and I will have to get together so you can show me the slides of what Mark Hinton owned."

"He called me." After giving Jace and Leni a glass of wine, Nick sat beside Leni. "I know it probably seems like we're keeping you in New York unnecessarily, but it's important that you know everything your dad owned so that if you decide not to take anything you know what you're refusing. Name the day and hour and I'll bring the laptop to Jace's condo or you can meet me here and we'll watch in the media room."

It suddenly hit her that everybody knew every step of her life. Danny had probably called Nick about the slides. Jace had called Nick to arrange for dinner and would have mentioned Charlotte was eager to meet Leni. And she knew Leni had already gone through this process—

Of course. That's why everyone appeared overly informed. They'd been through this once.

"Danny told me it will take days just to see the slides of what he owned."

Nick chuckled. "Your dad had tons of things."

Jace said, "Nothing says love of the water like thirty sets of Jet Skis."

"Not to mention the four beach houses and two lake houses."

Charlotte's mouth fell open. "Four beach houses?"

"Every beach house is different," Jace explained. "The house in the Florida Keys was all about fishing. Fiji was where Mark hid. Hawaii's just plain beautiful. And Ocean City was where he could get lost in the crowd."

Charlotte said, "Wow." But the feeling that something was off about this discussion surged through her again. Jace was awfully familiar with her dad's things. She supposed it could be knowledge gained while guarding him, but there was something about his tone of voice that said there was more. There was an affection he couldn't hide.

Her brain caught up with reality slowly. She wasn't supposed to like or trust people who were involved with her dad. Especially someone who was as close to her dad as Jace had been. Yet, she liked Jace. Instantly. And more than she'd ever liked anyone. But his connection to her dad should have dissolved any sort of romantic feelings. Just being *similar to* her dad had caused her to knock more than one guy out of her dating pool—

Confusion made her frown. Odd disjointed memories swamped her. Breaking up with men who were overly committed to their careers—because they reminded her of her dad. Not compromising. Not investigating. Not trying things. Just a cold, hard no to men who reminded her of her father—

Looking back over the short list of men she'd dated, men she'd slept with, even men she'd thought she could love, at some point every one of them had reminded her of her dad. Or, more appropriately, her mom's situation with her dad.

The room shimmied. Her brain stalled. Her whole dating life flashed before her eyes one more time just so she could be sure she was remembering correctly.

All these years, she'd believed seeing her mom's life had been a good thing. A warning that she didn't want to get involved with someone who'd hurt her like her dad had hurt her mom. But what if her dad's desertion and her mom's devotion had actually scarred her so much that she chased *everyone* off?

Never trusted?

Never let herself fall in love?

What if her father had caused her to nitpick every man until *no one* was good enough?

Even the idea that there might be "The One," with her standards so high most men didn't reach them, might have been a way to protect herself.

The thought left her breathless and angry. Not with her dad. With herself. All this time she'd thought she was strong, smart. But what if she'd simply been too scared to take a risk?

CHAPTER EIGHT

THEY LEFT NICK and Leni's penthouse around ten. Though the dinner conversation had been lively with Leni telling Charlotte about her plans for her hometown's restoration and revitalization, and Charlotte offering development and construction tips, Jace's instincts had shifted to red alert. Charlotte was smart, obviously liked Leni and Nick, but never said another personal word about herself.

He led her into the cold April night and to the limo. After they were tucked away in the backseat and the driver had pulled into traffic, he thought about asking her if she was okay, but his mind ventured to their kiss again. The power of it. The *fun* of it.

Normally, he kept on top of his client's moods, but this client was tricky because he really liked her. If she wanted to talk, he would let her. But maybe it wasn't so smart to nudge her to open up, to take them to that place where they realized how well they got along, how much they liked each other?

He stayed silent and so did she.

In his condo, she said good night. As he punched numbers in a keypad to activate the locks and alarms, she walked directly to her room.

Jace watched her, reminding himself there was nothing wrong with that. Her saying good night and going to her room while he secured the premises was typical bodyguard stuff.

The way it should be.

The next morning, keeping them within the context of bodyguard and client, he woke first, made eggs and toast and knocked on her door to tell her breakfast had been made but she reminded him she wasn't a breakfast person.

Fine. She was an adult. She also wasn't the kind of person who liked someone looking over her shoulder or telling her what to do. Still, her tone of voice had been so cool…

He shook off the sense that she was angry with him. She couldn't be. He hadn't done anything.

Except kiss her.

No. Technically, she'd kissed him. He'd simply taken a great kiss and made it better. And they'd talked about that. They were square. She was not angry with him. He was jumpy because she was quiet, but if he left her alone it would all even out.

He went to his office space, a desk in a nook in the master bedroom, got to work and came out after an hour for coffee. He expected to see evidence that she'd at least made herself a cup, too, but everything was exactly as he'd left it.

All right. That was enough. He'd ever seen her go a morning without coffee. Something was wrong and he needed to be on top of it.

He walked back the hall again and knocked on her door. "I made coffee."

"Thanks, but I'm fine."

"If you drink tea—" She hadn't the two days they were at her house, but an unexpected desperation had settled in his chest. If she were a normal client, he'd walk into her room and ask her point-blank what was wrong. But he couldn't sashay into her bedroom. It wasn't merely invasive...it was suggestive.

This is what he got for kissing her. Now everything was confused. He couldn't do what he knew he should do.

"I have tea bags in the second counter from the right."

"No, thanks."

He battled back the guilt. Okay. Yes. She'd been a bit weird during their conversation after the kiss, but she'd also gotten details of her dad's estate and met her half sister. Any of those things could have overwhelmed her enough that she'd withdrawn.

He squeezed his eyes shut. It didn't matter why she'd pulled back, why she wouldn't even drink his coffee. She had still withdrawn. And having her not talk was as bad as getting too friendly. It might seem okay that her mind was off somewhere, stuck on things she wasn't telling him. But he needed to have her attention. He needed to know she'd hear his orders. Not get bumped or shoved or even photographed because she hadn't heard him say, "Go this way," or "Turn that way."

He had to get them back on track. Things might be fine right now, but they had to be prepared. She had to talk to him. He had to talk to her. Just not about personal stuff.

He walked back to his bedroom nook. Even before he set his coffee on the small desk, his phone rang. Caller ID indicated it was one of his best men. Oswald Patterson, a team leader who was currently guarding a pop star.

"What's up, Oz?"

"We've got a problem with Seth Simon."

"Is he drunk?"

"Stayed out all night."

"Damn."

"He wants to go for a walk around the city. Meet his fans."

"He can't do that. Not drunk, anyway. His squeaky-clean image would go straight to hell after two minutes of him slurring his words and spitting on people."

"I know. I've barely kept him here since I sneaked him back into the hotel. And his concert's tonight. I need to make sure he goes to bed and stays there. There's no way in hell I can attend our staff meeting."

Jace groaned. "I forgot about the staff meeting." He paused a second. "Tell you what. We'll have our meeting in Seth's suite."

He clicked off the call, and sent a text informing the rest of his team leaders of the change of venue for the meeting. He picked up his laptop, pretty sure it was safe to leave Charlotte alone, but a thought stopped him.

Charlotte didn't understand why she'd need a bodyguard, a real bodyguard, not someone she treated like a friend? Maybe this meeting with his staff giving reports would change that?

He knocked on her bedroom door, but didn't wait for her answer, just entered. "Hey, I have my weekly Saturday staff meeting this afternoon. Wanna come with me?"

"You're leaving?"

The lightness in her voice didn't sit well. It almost sounded like she planned to make a break for it. "Yes, but I thought you'd want to come with me."

"Why would I want to go to a staff meeting?"

"To get out of the condo? To hear some interesting stories from my guys? We're providing security for a singer who's giving a concert tonight." He shrugged. "We're actually having the meeting in his suite."

"So, I'd meet a rock star?"

"He's more pop than rock, but you could call him a rock star."

"Who is he?"

"Seth Simon."

Her eyes widened. Her mouth fell open. "Seth Simon, the cutie pie?"

"You're about to find out he's not so cute."

She laughed. "That might be even more fun."

"You just have to take a vow of silence."

She frowned. "So, I'm back to being a spy?"

"You were never a spy. Spies have missions. People who guard just watch. We don't try to steal military secrets or corporate secrets or any kind of secrets at all." He grinned. "But we do see and hear some great stuff. And you have to promise to keep it confidential."

"You know what? I'm in, anyway. It's Saturday and I'll only get reports from jobsites that are on overtime and then not until after dark." She grabbed her leather jacket. "And I'll keep Seth Simon's supposed secrets. You're his security company, responsible for him. I'm guessing you think anything he does that's outside your box is bad behavior. I'm a civilian. I understand when someone wants to have fun. The poor guy probably flushed the toilet wrong and your team jumped. I'm guessing I'll love him. The man is adorable."

He followed her to the front door, then the elevator. The doors opened and they stepped inside.

"We'll see if you still think he's adorable after twenty minutes."

A laugh bubbled from her, but she caught it. Stopped it before it could fully fill the air.

His chest bunched. He hated the distance she'd put between them. He knew it was necessary, but she didn't have to be a totally different person. "It's okay to laugh."

"That was an aberration. I don't want to laugh."

"A lot happened yesterday. Danny told you things that probably blew your mind. Then you met Leni, and if meeting your sister for the first time wasn't unusual enough, you saw a lifestyle so different from your own that it might have confused you. And somehow you found a way to blame me for all of it when none of it's my fault. I'm just your bodyguard."

Their gazes connected. Confusion filled her blue eyes.

"Charlotte, we have to communicate. Out there in the big, wide, wonderful world, your life could be in jeopardy. It's my job to see problems and avoid them. I can't do that if you won't look at me or talk to me."

She snorted. "Right. This is actually our real area of disagreement. You think I'm in danger. I think I'm perfectly safe. There are eight million people in this city. More than ten million during the day when workers commute in. I'm like a bean in a big bag of beans. Yet somehow you think I stick out."

"You do. But not in the way you think and not to everyone."

She shook her head. "You're crazy."

"Okay. I can handle you thinking I'm crazy. But we need to talk. If it helps going back to the way we were before the kiss, we could do that."

The elevator door opened. "You mean talk like friends?"

"Yeah."

"I thought that screwed up your bodyguard mojo."

"In some ways." He smiled. "But I like you. We always find interesting things to talk about."

Her eyes changed, softened, and she swallowed.

"I promise nothing will happen like that kiss again."

Her eyebrows rose.

He laughed. "Just get out of the elevator."

With a breath she stepped into the lobby, strode to the revolving door and then the limo.

He opened the door for her. "Now that we have that settled, we'll have some fun this afternoon."

Her entire countenance changed. "Yeah. Meeting a rock star. I like this part of your job."

"Just don't get in the way."

"*Moi?*" she asked innocently, her eyes widening comically.

He groaned. "Get in the limo."

* * *

As Charlotte expected, Seth Simon was staying in the penthouse suite of an elegant hotel. She didn't care that she wore a sweater and jeans and looked like an average fan. The man was a superstar. She didn't want to marry him. She just wanted to meet him, flirt a little, hear stories about how he came up with his beautiful, heartrending songs.

And then brag to her friends.

The thought of it made her giddy as they rode the elevator to the suite. The door opened on opulence so magnificent she had to work to catch her breath. Ultramodern furniture sat on shiny white floors. In the back, a baby grand piano stood in front of a wall of windows. She could picture Seth sitting there, a lone soul with the big city as a backdrop, singing his gut-wrenching songs about longing for real love.

Her heart fluttered.

A twentysomething kid wearing jeans and a black T-shirt with enough tattoos to be an art gallery came into the main area.

Jace said, "Charlotte, this is Oz Patterson, one of my best men. Oz, this is Charlotte Fillion, also a client."

Charlotte reached out and shook his hand. "So, you're guarding Seth Simon!"

"More like babysitting," Oz said. "Guys are in the conference room."

Charlotte looked around in awe again. "This suite has a conference room?"

"Of course."

"Wow. Where's Seth?"

"Sleeping off one hell of a night last night."

Charlotte gaped at Oz. "He was drunk?"

"As a monkey."

Jace snorted. "I told you he's not what you think."

"But he's sleeping! I came here to meet him."

"And you will. He'll be awake before you know it. He doesn't really sleep. Just catnaps." He directed her back a hall to the right. "Wait in the conference room with us."

She followed him with a sigh. "You just want me to get introduced to your crew so I'll see they're harmless and agree to let one of them guard me when I go back to Pittsburgh."

Jace laughed. "I thought you didn't want a guard."

"I don't!"

They stepped into the conference room area where pots of coffee in silver carafes sat spaced apart in a line on the long table.

Jace's five team leaders rose as Charlotte entered the room, but she stopped dead in her tracks. Two tall, handsome men wore suits. One guy and the woman to his right wore jeans. The woman wore a sweater with hers. The guy had on a plaid work shirt. The fifth guy looked like he'd pulled his clothes out of a ragbag.

Jace walked to the head of the table. "This is Charlotte Fillion, a client. I thought she'd enjoy sitting in on a meeting and meeting Seth Simon."

All five groaned.

Charlotte ambled to a chair at the far end of the table. "He can't be that bad."

One of the guys in a suit rolled his eyes. "He's Satan."

Charlotte laughed. "No. He's not. He's cute and honest and likable."

Opening his laptop, Jace said, "His songs are cute and honest and likable. He is not."

"So, the whole thing he does onstage, with finding a girl and singing to her and making space for kids in wheelchairs...that's just an act."

The men laughed. The woman snorted in disgust.

"Wow."

Jace introduced people as he pointed at them. "Elizabeth Nelson, Carter Davis, Blake Regan, Isaac Tanner and you met Oz."

Charlotte politely said, "Nice to meet you all," even though she expected to be bored and was totally annoyed that her reason for coming here was asleep.

Jace opened the meeting. "This week's assignments are on your phones. Each of your team members will get their schedules tonight with your squad leaders getting them about an hour before in case they have questions or problems."

Confused, Charlotte held up her hand and said, "Wait. These five people are your team leaders."

One of Jace's eyebrows rose. She wasn't sure if he was angry that she had a question or angry that she'd interrupted. She kept going, anyway.

"Then each of you supervises a group of squad leaders," she said, pointing at the five people sitting at the table. "And they supervisor your basic bodyguards?"

They all said, "Yes," or "Exactly," or some form of affirmation.

She peered up at Jace at the far, far end of the very long table. "Just how many people do you employ?"

"Probably as many as you supervise."

"I have hundreds of people under me!"

"So do I." He gestured to Elizabeth. "Liz has almost two hundred in her group alone."

"We do 24/7 protection for a large New England family. Five guards on the compound grounds, two watching monitors, three shifts a day, drivers and personal guards when they travel," Liz said proudly. "And that's just one client."

"That's also because they have a big family," Jace said. "Grandparents, parents, six kids and their husbands or wives and babies."

Impressed, Charlotte sat back. "Okay, then."

She let him proceed with his business because

he had her attention. She watched him discuss strategy, hear reports on the progress of new hires and engage in a lively debate with Carter over his choice of route through the city for yet another rock star.

"Excuse me," she interrupted again. "You have more than one rock star client?"

Jace looked at her. "Word gets around that we're good."

She leaned her elbow on the table, studying him. The devil in her wanted to say, "I'll bet you are." But there was more than one meaning to that and she wasn't entirely sure which one she meant. She'd thought it was masterful that he'd gotten the right clothes to her house for working on the jobsite? Watching him plan, critique and engage his employees almost made her breathless.

This was the point when her brain always shimmied. Told her to run. Reminded her that she couldn't or shouldn't like someone who was in any way, shape or form similar to or connected to her father. For the first time in her adult life she recognized the fear that eased its way into her thoughts, made her want to find a fault, pick Jace apart and back away.

But this time she didn't have to. Jace didn't want her.

Maybe that was why she could see her own side of things so clearly. Every other relationship, she was the one doing the rejecting. This time, Jace had rejected her.

A funny feeling filled her chest. It was equal parts of odd and amazing to be seeing her behavior so clearly. But it was also incredibly sad that he didn't want to follow through with what they felt.

But if he did, if he'd been the one to kiss her, would she be backing off, finding fault, looking for the fastest way to get away from him?

It angered her to think about it but being angry with herself was foolish. Once a person recognized a bad behavior it was smarter to fix it than indulge useless emotions.

But how could she fix this? She couldn't go after a man who didn't want her.

An hour into the meeting, the conference room door opened. Seth Simon walked in—naked.

"I need a burrito."

Without looking up, Jace said, "You need pants."

Oz pulled out his phone. "I'll call room service."

Jace said, "Get a half dozen bottles of water, too. It's time he started hydrating so he'll have a voice tonight."

The naked rock star standing no more than twenty feet away should have had her full attention. Instead, she stared at Jace. His instincts were so good he didn't even have to glance at Seth Simon to know he was naked.

"I hate water."

Jace shook his head. "Fine. Have dry vocal cords. Disappoint your fans. None of that would surprise me."

"You suck as a security service."

"No, we don't, or you'd fire us." Jace nodded to Oz. "Order the burrito and the water, then get him back to bed."

Oz rose. Seth Simon sighed but he spotted Charlotte and his face lit as he walked toward her. "And who is this? My new guard?"

She should have gasped with joy. Maybe even fought a giggle. But her favorite singer was naked. And being a pain in the ass.

Giving Oz a pointed look, Jace said only, "No. Charlotte is not your new guard."

"She's tall enough and looks sturdy."

Charlotte gaped at him, all thoughts of being impressed by him gone. Being crude was bad enough. But calling her sturdy? That was nineteenth-century insulting. "What am I? A horse?"

"And I love her sense of humor! Please, please, please can I have her?"

"Have me?" She stood up and towered over him. "This isn't the Old West. Men don't choose a woman and run off with her."

Looking confused and wobbly, he stared at her. Oz came over, grabbed his arm and guided him out of the room.

Charlotte watched them leave. "I guess it's true what they say about meeting your idols."

All four of Jace's remaining supervisors laughed.

Jace closed his laptop. "We're done, anyway. Anybody else want a burrito?"

Liz had a lunch meeting with the mother of one of her clients. Carter, Blake and Isaac scrambled to the door with various excuses and were in the elevator in what seemed to be seconds.

"A client like Seth is potential poison," Jace said as he rose from his seat. "That's why they all jetted out of here."

"Poison?"

"Sure. No one wants him to remember their names. He's going to fire us eventually in one of his tantrums and I probably won't argue. I'll gather my guys and leave."

"How's that poison?"

"He'll bad-mouth us." He stopped her before she headed up the hall. "Everybody has the same opinion of him you had before you met him. His songs make everyone think he's a great guy. So, when he tries to ruin our reputation on social media most people will believe him."

"Then why take him as a client?"

"He needs us."

Skeptical, she narrowed her eyes. "Really? That's why you're here?"

"I'd guard him forever, keep him hydrated and

his reputation intact because deep down he really is the lost soul he sings about. He overcompensates by being a jackass. But pretty soon, he's going to get in a mood and dump us. Then at least I'll know I did what I could for him."

Her heart softened. "You're a nice guy." She should have realized it when he extended condolences to her mother on Mark's death, but it only fully hit her now.

Jace laughed. "I'm a nice guy to a point. No matter how much I want to protect him, I won't let him hurt us. I've planned for the inevitable social media war."

Charlotte tilted her head and studied him. It was no wonder she liked him. He wasn't just muscles, sex appeal and bossy. He was a genuinely good person.

He shrugged. "You would plan for it, too."

She would. If she and Jace ever started a business together, they would be invincible.

If they started a romance, they'd be red hot and fierce.

She had to stop thinking that way. Because for the first time in her life, someone she was interested in didn't want her—

It was confusing and annoying. Mostly because she knew she shouldn't start something with a man who was only trying to do his job.

She pulled in a breath, clueless about what all this meant. She was twenty-eight, had never been dumped, had always been the one to break things off. Under normal circumstances, she'd think life was telling her she should break the cycle with Jace—

But he was her bodyguard.

And didn't want her.

They walked up the hall. Room service arrived with a bucket of bottles of water on ice and what looked like a mountain of burritos.

Wearing a robe now, Seth lounged on the sofa. He gave Charlotte the killer smile he was famous for, the one that made him look sexy in an innocent boy-next-door way.

"Sorry about the whole no-clothes thing." He laughed. "I sometimes like to rattle the team."

His voice had softened. His face appeared almost angelic. She'd think she was crazy, that she'd somehow misinterpreted what had happened when he'd stepped into the conference room, if she hadn't witnessed it for herself and didn't trust Jace enough to believe everything he said.

Her breath caught. Dear God. She *trusted* Jace?

Yeah. Of course she did. Actually, that was the missing link. The reason she couldn't shake the attraction the way she'd shaken off her attractions before this.

She didn't merely like him. She wasn't just attracted to him. She trusted him.

None of which mattered. He wasn't interested.

"I'd love it if you'd join me for lunch."

Seth Simon's angelic voice, the voice that sounded like it came from heaven, interrupted her thoughts.

She glanced at Jace, who gave her a nod telling her the decision was hers. The comparison that resulted was almost comical. Next to strong, smart, disciplined, masterful Jace, Seth Simon was…weird.

"Sorry, Seth." She gave him *her* best smile. The one that fooled wayward employees and subcontractors into thinking they weren't on thin ice with her. "But I have to get back to my suite to make some calls."

"Too bad." His eyes shadowed.

He could certainly pull out the charm when he needed it.

Seth snapped his fingers. "I know! Come to my show tonight." He pushed off the sofa and headed for the piano by the wall of window. Grabbing two tickets from the bench seat, he turned to her. "You and Jace."

The guy might be a fake. But she did love his music. "You know what? I'd like that."

Seth said, "Those tickets come with backstage passes that you'll get at the door."

Truly touched, she took the tickets. "Thank you."

Genuine, innocent, he nodded. "You're welcome."

Jace pressed the button for the elevator door to open. "Go eat your burrito and drink that water."

Seth laughed. "Will do, boss."

Jace snorted as the elevator door opened. Charlotte stepped inside and even gave Seth a little wave as the doors closed.

"Are you sure he's more evil than good?"

"The good is an act. Trust me."

She pulled in an uncomfortable breath. There was that word again. Trust. Realizing they were back to being friendly, and that she was facing an attraction to a man in a totally different way than she ever had, her chest tightened. Without the crutch of comparing him to her dad, being able to walk away before she got hurt, she was shaky, vulnerable.

Jace shook his head. "Such an act, giving you backstage passes."

"I thought it was a nice way for him to make up for being an ass at first."

Jace peered at her. "I run his security team. I print those backstage passes."

"Oh." Yet he hadn't embarrassed Seth when he'd made what he'd thought was a grand gesture. He also hadn't yelled at him for being naked. He'd told him to put on pants. And he worried about his performance that night…reminding him to hydrate.

Jace MacDonald was an interesting, complicated man, and the thought of spending more time with him, actually being in a relationship with him, was equal parts frightening and wonderful.

But for once in her life, she wasn't calling the shots. He was. And he was saying no to anything happening between them.

CHAPTER NINE

CHARLOTTE DRESSED FOR the concert in a pair of skinny jeans and her leather jacket, looking as she always did, tall and sleek with a splash of cool when she put on her sunglasses. Jace directed her to the door of his condo without breaking out of bodyguard mode, though his heart stuttered. She was sexy as hell.

For the first time since he'd chosen his profession, he felt out of step with it. He'd never been as attracted to or as in tune with a client and every instinct he had was screaming that it was wrong that he couldn't touch her. Couldn't laugh with her. Couldn't talk about anything but her dad, the estate, how she would need protection.

Because protecting her was his job.

Nothing else.

And that felt wrong, too.

They arrived twenty minutes before the show. As Jace's crew handled Seth, Jace stayed with Charlotte. She might not stand out at a concert, but she was still his responsibility.

The opening act finished. Seth took the stage. He didn't have a big band behind him. No special effects. Just himself, a guitar and that sweet angelic face of his that had made him millions.

He sat on the tall stool, strummed the guitar to tune it, made friends with the audience who clapped and cheered and yelled, "We love you, Seth!"

Jace watched it all, not sure if he was proud of Seth for using his talent or confused about how someone could be one way onstage and exactly the opposite in real life.

Two of the guys from the opening act walked over to Jace and Charlotte, who stood just out of the sight lines off the stage. One cracked open a beer. The other had a whiskey bottle in his hand.

Still in costume—baggy shirts and low-riding print pants with wide legs—they looked like refugees from a hair band in the 1990s.

The first one said, "Evening, mates."

Jace nodded. "Evening."

Charlotte smiled.

The tall one with perfect teeth faced Charlotte. "So, what agency are you with?"

Seth's soft mellow music in the background didn't preclude conversation so Jace wasn't surprised when she answered.

"I'm not sure what you mean."

"You model, right?"

Charlotte laughed. "No. I'm a vice president in a development company."

He grinned. "A big shot."

She laughed again.

Seth finished one song and started another, but he stopped abruptly after only a few chords. "You know what? This is such an emotional song for me, I think I want to be closer to you all. Let me move this stool up a few feet."

The audience cheer sounded like a roar of thunder. Feet stomped. Whistles sounded.

He slid off the seat, but his foot caught, and he fell forward. Jace was on the stage and in front of him in seconds. He didn't prevent his fall, but he was there in time to help him up and ensure he was okay.

Charlotte watched it all, her heart in her throat. She'd developed a theory about Seth. That he was a lost soul and he needed someone like Jace. With every fiber of his being Jace was a protector. Happy to help him.

"So, while that simpleton's melting his way into women's panties by pretending to be wounded, what do you say we go back to the dressing room and unpack the hard stuff?"

Charlotte turned to the member of the opening act who had spoken. "What? Hard stuff?" She shook her head. "Guys, I drink a beer now and again. Maybe have a glass of wine. But that's as far as I go."

Band member number one caught her arm. "Come on. That's nonsense. Everybody likes to party."

"Not me," she said, yanking on her arm, but his grip was firm. She didn't like this guy or his smarmy friend. With their scarf headbands and wide-leg printed pants they looked like they shopped at Steven Tyler's garage sale. For once, she was glad to be under Jace's care. "Besides, I'm with Jace."

"That old stick in the mud?" He laughed. "You need to spend some time with a real man. See what fun is."

The obvious direction of his thoughts made her stomach turn. His pupils were dilated. His breath stank of whiskey. But his grip was almost superhuman.

Behind her the crowd broke into applause. The creep tightened his hold on her arm and shoved her to the right. "Let's go."

She tried to stand her ground, but her feet slid in the direction he dragged her. "No!"

His friend came around to the side, caught her other arm and all but lifted her off the floor.

"Jace!"

She screamed his name but knew her voice would be swallowed by the noise of the crowd.

Close to the back now, almost at the elevator, they weren't even in a position that Jace could see her.

Jace returned from the stage, shaking his head, laughing at how smoothly Seth had gotten beyond his fall by introducing Jace and making him take a bow for helping him.

He began to say, "Did you see—?"

But Charlotte was nowhere in sight. Panic rose from his stomach to fill his chest. He raced to the side, pushing his way through the small crowd of roadies, press and people who'd been granted backstage passes, and saw her with the musicians from the opening act. Each held one of her arms and she was struggling.

He took off running and caught them just before they reached the lift to the lower area and the dressing rooms. He yanked the skinny lead singer away from her and would have punched the guitarist, but his eyes widened, and he dropped her arm.

He faced the lead singer. "What the hell are you doing?"

"Just trying to have some fun, mate."

"The lady didn't want to go with you."

He looked affronted. "I planned on convincing her." A drunken grin lifted his lips. "I can be very persuasive."

Jace fought the urge to haul off and hit him. "You can be a piece of crap. You know that?"

He caught Charlotte close. "And for God's sake, get a stylist. The '90s are over."

He headed toward the stage. "Are you okay?"

"I'm fine. They rattled me. But I'm fine."

She didn't look fine. Her face was pasty white. Her eyes were shiny and confused.

He tapped his earpiece. "Oz, I'm leaving with Charlotte. Get someone back here pronto. And alert security about the opening act. Tell them they tried to accost a woman and we want them off-site. Also call Seth's manager and tell him that Seth never works with these two again."

The word "Affirmative" came through his com.

He motioned for Charlotte to turn right and walk with him. They went down the back stairs and made their way through a maze of corridors and tunnels before they reached the door, walked outside and to Jace's limo.

They got in and he told the driver to take them to his condo.

Charlotte leaned back on the seat and closed her eyes. After about ten minutes, she said, "That was stupid."

"Which part?"

"Their behavior." She sat up again. "The fact that I couldn't get away from them. Both." She made a sound of disgust. "I'm a very strong person. They should not have been able to outmaneuver me that way."

"You have the strength," Jace said, his heart

finally settling down now that they were close to home. "But not the moves."

She narrowed her eyes at him. "Moves? What are we? Dancing?"

He laughed. Her face was no longer pasty. Her humor was back. "In a way."

She sniffed.

"Seriously. If you know the right moves, you can get yourself out of situations like that."

"And here I thought you'd be glad something had happened to show me that I needed a bodyguard."

"You say you don't want one."

"I don't."

"And in my world the customer is the boss." He met the gaze of her pretty blue eyes. "But that doesn't mean I won't worry about you."

He could tell she almost said something about being fine. But they both knew she wasn't. The incident had shaken her. Only a fool would pretend otherwise. Charlotte wasn't a fool.

But he saw more. Her eyes softened when he'd said he'd worry about her. It hit him oddly too. They'd only been together a few days, and in another few days they'd part. Maybe never to see each other again.

The mere thought did funny things to his heart. He told it to settle down and brought the conversation back on track, to the real problem they needed to discuss.

"Since what you say goes, and you're walking away from protection, I think we should use some of your time with me teaching you a few easy defensive moves."

She inclined her head in agreement. "Maybe it wouldn't be a bad idea for you to teach me a few of the difficult moves, too."

Her voice held a slight quaver that told him she'd been a little more upset than she'd wanted him to believe. That caused the funny floating feeling in his heart again. If he let himself picture her being accosted when he wasn't around, his brain would explode.

"Okay, as soon as we get inside, we'll both change into sweats and a T-shirt and I'll show you some really effective moves."

She nodded. "Sounds good."

They reached his condo building and were quiet as they entered the lobby and rode the elevator. They walked back to their rooms and in less than five minutes both were standing in the center of his living area, dressed for the lessons.

Looking antsy, she said, "It's so tidy here. I'm afraid we'll break a lamp."

"What do you think we're going to do?"

"Aren't you going to show me how to lob someone over my shoulder while yelling, *Hy-ya!*"

He laughed. "No. But there is some movement." He glanced around. "I'll tell you what. There's a big open space in the master bedroom. Let's go there."

She followed him back to his room and they walked inside. "Nice. Very horror film decor."

He flicked on a few extra lights. "I work back here. The darkness makes me feel like it's totally private."

"The fact that you're thirty stories up and only have one other tenant on your floor should actually manage that."

She looked lean and supple in her yoga pants and white T-shirt. Very bendy. Like someone who could karate kick you in the face, then step back and do fifty squats. She should be extremely easy to teach.

He guided them to stand in the center of an area rug he'd always thought had no purpose until just now. It was large enough and thick enough to act like a mat.

"Fine. Whatever. Do you want to learn or not?"

She raised her hands in surrender. "I'm ready."

"Okay, first order of business. Less is more. If you can kick your assailant in the nuts and disable him…run. That's your best defense."

"I'm a good runner." She held out a leg. "Long legs. A benefit of being tall."

With her slender form outlined in the tight clothes, he saw other benefits, but quickly shifted his mind elsewhere.

"If you don't get a chance to kick him in the

privates, or if he or she is coming at you, there are a few moves to protect yourself." He took a defensive stance. "For instance, if someone punches you, grab the elbow of the arm coming toward you—" He caught her elbow with one hand and made a fist with the other. "Then use your free hand to punch them in the stomach."

She made an awkward attempt at mimicking what he'd shown her.

"That's pretty good. But the trick is to use your whole arm. Your whole upper body."

He took the stance again. "Okay. Let's try something else. If someone comes toward you to grab you like this—" he reached toward her with both arms "—you catch their hands and flip them down...as you kick them in the nuts."

She laughed. "So, what you're consistently saying is I have to do two things at once."

He didn't see anything funny in anything he'd said. "Yes. They'll be expecting one move. You do two. Plus, flipping down their hands is more of a distraction, so they don't notice you're about to kick them."

He held out his hands. "Let's try. Grab my hands, then do the initial movements of the kick, but don't actually kick me."

She swallowed back a laugh. "Yeah. I'm glad you set some boundaries because I did not want to kick you there."

She caught his hands, turned them down to shove them away, then did a partial kick.

"That wasn't bad."

She danced around like a prizefighter. "Show me something else."

"Let's try the thing where you block the punch, but this time use your shoulder to knock them back."

She nodded eagerly. He faked a punch. She blocked it, but her shoulder knock was weak.

"Try again."

She did and was equally unsuccessful.

He walked behind her. "Here's the deal. When people are struggling, their instinct is to use their hands. Block. Shove. Push. All they think of is hands."

She nodded.

"Raise your right arm."

She did.

"Bend it at the elbow."

She bent it.

He lifted his hand to her fingers. "This is what you have at your disposal. Fingers to jab in someone's eye. Hands to slap. Forearms to block." His hands followed his words, drifting from her fingers to her wrist to her forearm. "Elbow. Great again for jabs. Upper arms, stronger than forearms. And shoulders." He'd been following the inside of her smooth, silky arm, not realizing he wouldn't end up at her shoulder but right above her breast. He moved his hand quickly to her shoulder, but instinct wanted him to slide down along the sides of her breasts to her ribs to her stomach to the soft flare of her hips.

His breath stuttered. His bedroom grew silent.

His *bedroom*. What the hell had he been thinking, bringing her here? Sure, there was more space. But—

He cleared his throat. "Anyway, let's practice some of that."

He stepped away and walked in front of her again, but when he turned to face her, her eyes were bright, her lips parted.

Damn. He shouldn't have touched her—

But his ego puffed a little. His innocent touches had her breathing funny, too—

Not important.

"So, what you need to learn is to use your upper body like a weapon."

Eyes serious and confused, she nodded.

"Do you think you can barrel into me with a shoulder?"

She nodded.

He took the stance. "Okay, so I'm a kidnapper. You're on your way to a restaurant, reading a text from the person you're meeting. You look up and here I am, ready to grab you and toss you into this van."

He pointed to the right where he wanted her

to imagine a van. Her gaze ambled over and one eyebrow rose.

She should have made a smart remark about the pretend van. Instead, her shiny blue eyes met his.

He swallowed. He'd just invited her to plow into him, when the feel of her skin had him about crazy. He had no idea what would happen when her entire body bumped into his.

He pointed at his rib cage. "Your goal is to hit me here." He motioned to the top of his stomach. "Or here."

She started her prizefighter dance again. "With my shoulder."

"Yes. Hit me really hard with this part of your shoulder." He grabbed the bony part of his own shoulder. "Hard enough that I will grunt and be caught off guard."

She nodded again.

"Okay. You're on your way into a restaurant, looking at your phone, you glance up and there I am. Bend, shift your shoulder to the front and ram into me."

She did as he asked but the hit was weak.

He brought her out of her bent posture. "You need to focus your power from here..." He motioned from her stomach, up her chest. His hands were centimeters away from her belly, her ribs, her breasts.

He swallowed. "To here."

She blinked at him.

Time spun out with them inches away from each other, holding their breaths, just wanting to touch the forbidden fruit that was always in front of them, always tormenting them.

She took a step toward him.

He took a step toward her.

He wasn't entirely sure who made the first move but the next thing he knew they were kissing.

CHAPTER TEN

FAMILIAR FEAR RACED through Charlotte. The fear that he was just using her. The fear that he'd leave her. But she stopped it. There was no place for fear in what she felt for Jace. Even if this was a one-night stand, she wanted it. It was time to change the way she felt about everything. Time to let go of the past. Time to stop thinking of everything in terms of her dad. Fight the fear. And live her life.

She reached for the bottom of Jace's shirt and yanked it up, shifting away from their kiss only long enough to pull it over his head and toss it away.

"Charlotte—"

"Stop. Don't talk us out of this. I like you. You like me. We both want this." And for once she wanted to be rid of the fear, to look it in the eye and tell it it didn't matter. That she'd survive a little pain because the pleasure would be worth it.

She must have convinced him because he kissed

her again. His mouth moved over hers hungrily and she responded equally greedily. Terrible reminders of being abandoned flitted through her brain. She blocked them. Her entire life had been spent being worried about the future. She desperately needed to live in the moment.

He grabbed the hem of her T-shirt and yanked it up as she stepped back far enough that he could pull it over her head. When they were breast to chest, her eyes drifted shut. With only the thin lace of her bra between them, the sensations passing through her stole her breath. She'd made love with men before but never one she was so attracted to. Never someone she wanted so much, even though she knew this wasn't permanent. In a few days or weeks, he'd be out of her life.

But that was the point. Not everything had to last forever. Some things were short-term. For enjoyment.

He reached behind her and unhooked her bra. Their gazes caught as if each gave the other one last chance to back away. But neither moved until Jace slid his hand around her neck, pulled her close and kissed her as if he'd been starving for her his entire life.

Everything after that happened in a rush. A riot of touches and tastes, smooth caresses and kisses so long and deep she could have drowned in them. His silky soft burgundy-colored sheets added to the pleasure and she forgot all about her life, her fears, and lived in the sinfully sexy moment with the strongest yet somehow nicest man she'd ever met.

Jace woke the next morning wrapped around Charlotte. He gave himself thirty seconds to enjoy it—to soak in the feeling of her sleek shape pressed against his—then he squeezed his eyes shut.

He'd slept with a client. He'd done that only once before to devastating consequences. Charlotte wasn't the kind of woman to write a tell-all book. But sleeping with a client was against rule number one for security people. No matter how good, no matter how much they'd both wanted this to happen, it had been wrong.

His instinct was to rain kisses from her shoulders to her hips, to flip her over and do everything they'd done the night before, this time in the light when he could fully appreciate her.

His brain told him to get up, get a shower and go to the kitchen…all without waking her because he had to do damage control and he needed to think this through.

He managed to slide out of bed without disturbing her. He did allow himself a sigh of regret when he looked at her, her beautiful yellow hair spread out on his pillow, her creamy shoulders a stark contrast to his wine-colored sheets. After those sixty seconds, though, he headed for the master bath.

He showered but left his hair wet so he didn't have to run the hair dryer, which sounded like a jet engine and would wake her. He found sweats and a T-shirt in the walk-in closet/dressing room and tiptoed out into the hall.

The night before, they'd been cocooned in a world so private everything that happened between them had felt sacred, right. He'd been terrified when he hadn't seen her when he came off the stage from helping Seth Simon. He'd thought teaching her self-defense would ease the pounding of his heart and his worry over how easily something could happen to her. It hadn't. He'd never felt that kind of fear for a client, and when they'd started touching and her soft skin had been a reminder that she was safe, the relief had nearly overwhelmed him. It had certainly blotted out his better judgment.

In the kitchen, he made a pot of coffee and drank two cups before she finally found him. Dressed in her sweats and T-shirt from the day before, she rounded the island that bridged the living area and kitchen, slid her arms around his neck and kissed him.

Oh, God. It was the best kiss he'd had in years. Maybe decades. His body woke. His mind flooded with good ideas. But his left brain cleared its throat and reminded him that his entire life had been invested in his security company and he couldn't lose it all because he had the hots for a client.

He pulled back. She smiled at him. "Good morning, stud."

Even as his ego puffed out its chest, he winced. "Don't call me that. We shouldn't have slept together. You're a client."

Her forehead bunched. "Seriously? I mean, I know you said before that we shouldn't get involved. But this whole thing between us is different. I'm not your ordinary client."

He pulled back, away from her. "No kidding. Except you not being an ordinary client isn't because we like each other. Do you have any idea how much this estate is worth? I'm not just responsible for the heirs. My company is responsible for security systems in houses and vehicles, for security checks twice a month to make sure alarms are working and twice a year to make sure nothing has gone missing. We guarded your dad, his jobsites, his offices…"

She studied him a second. "So, combining what I saw yesterday with your supervisors to what you just said, I'm going to guess my dad's property is half your work."

"Yes."

"If you lose the estate as a client, your company loses half its value."

"In the snap of one person's fingers."

Her head tilted. "What does that have to do with you and me?"

"You're a client." He said it weakly. Because she already knew it. But it was still the crux of why sleeping with her had been the stupidest thing he'd ever done, even though it had also been the most wonderful.

He took a breath. "I'm your bodyguard. The great big, general guiding principle, first rule of bodyguards, is that you don't sleep with a client."

"Humph. I thought you would say the first rule is not to get personally involved because that would include all genders and ages."

He put his attention on the coffeepot and off her sweet butt. "You know I have to get personally involved."

"Just not too personally involved."

He peeked at her. "There has to be a line drawn in the sand."

"I'm not sure I understand why. If sleeping together makes me happy, keeps me from being bored, predisposes me to following your orders because I now think you're adorable when you boss me around...how is that bad?"

"Because I can't be distracted."

She laughed. "Are you saying you're blinded by my beauty?"

He groaned. "It's more than that. It's more like being with you pulls me out of a mind-set I need, away from the focus I need." He took a breath.

"But if you want to make this personal, there are other very good reasons why us messing around is wrong. For one, you don't know me."

"Because we've only been in each other's lives a few days. I'm sure we'll—"

"I'm divorced."

That stopped her. "Oh."

"And my wife cheated with my best friend."

"Oh."

That "oh" was longer, and her tone of voice told him she understood the depth of that kind of betrayal.

She considered that for a second before she said, "A relationship for you wouldn't be a simple, easy thing."

"No. But there's more." He pulled in a quiet breath. "I ran into my ex and former best friend— the guy she ultimately married—about two years later, right when my business was exploding. I was guarding the extremely spoiled thirty-year-old daughter of a client, and when we ran into my ex, Misha figured out what was going on pretty quickly."

Charlotte leaned against a cabinet. "That sounds like a good thing."

"I thought it was, too, because she slid her arm under mine and pretended that we were an item. There she was—gorgeous, obviously wealthy— with me in my suit and silk tie, and we looked like the kind of couple that ends up in a magazine."

She sniffed a laugh.

"When we got back in the limo, we kept up the game that we were dating. Laughing because it sure as hell had been good for my ego to be with someone when I ran into my ex, her new husband and their baby. But then we took the game too far."

"So, you didn't just kiss a client before. You slept with her."

"Only once. I learned my lesson when her dad disinherited her, and she decided to make money by writing a tell-all book."

Charlotte winced. "Ouch."

"We slept together only that one time, but she exaggerated. The way she wrote about it I was the aggressor and it took some..." He cleared his throat. "Coaxing for her to give in." He pulled in another breath. "Those couple of pages in her book rocked the trust of most of my best clients. I lost some. Sleeping with someone you're guarding isn't just an oops. It's a breach of trust."

"How can it be a breach of trust for us when I was as involved as you were?"

"Things change. Feelings change. What seemed like a good idea last night might someday seem like the stupidest thing you ever did."

"Or I might need the scintillating situation to perk up my tell-all book."

"Yes."

She gaped at him. "Seriously? I look like the kind of person to write a tell-all book?"

"It doesn't matter. My job is to protect you."

"And you've been attracted to me all along and still done a great job." She tilted her head as she studied him. "Our situation is different."

Her cell phone rang.

"Damn it!" She yanked it from the back pocket of her sweats, mumbling, "A building better have fallen down overnight for a foreman to call me this early." She frowned. "It's not one of my guys." She glanced at Jace. "It's my mom. I have to take it."

Jace said, "Sure. Absolutely." But when she left the room, he called himself all kinds of names. Most of what she'd said was true. She was different. And he hadn't neglected his duties up to now, even though he'd been ridiculously attracted to her. In fact, what he felt for her sent a whoosh of supercharged desire to make sure nothing happened to her.

But those also felt like excuses. He'd lost control the night before because he'd been so afraid for her.

And that loss of control *was* a direct result of being attracted to her, liking her, connecting to her on a level he didn't with other clients.

She popped out of the hall and into the open area, looking as confused as he felt. "My mother is at LaGuardia."

"The airport?"

"You know another LaGuardia?"

"Does she have a ride?"

"She said she could catch a cab, but I told her to stay put. You'd probably send a limo."

He grabbed his phone and started texting. "Did she give you flight info?"

"Yes." She rattled off her mom's flight and which baggage claim area she was in.

Jace texted that to one of his drivers. "Someone will be there in thirty minutes or so, depending on traffic. Text her and tell her to get some coffee or something but be at her baggage claim area in thirty minutes."

"Great." She winced, looking sheepish. "Apparently in our last phone conversation, I gave her the impression I was bored. So, she decided this would make a good girls' trip."

His heart stuttered, even as his left brain sighed with relief that her mother would be around to send them both to neutral corners, no more long glances, no teasing, no kissing and absolutely no way they could sleep together. Maybe with that distance, the next time he got an opportunity to talk to her, she would actually hear what he was saying. That being attracted might be natural but acting on it was wrong.

"I think having your mom here is a good thing."

"Sure. It's particularly good to have my mom here if you insist that we're sticking to your plan of going back to bodyguard and newly found heiress and not following through on something I considered three steps above great."

"I'm insisting. Charlotte. I know you don't understand how much danger you are in, but anyone could be a fanatic with a gun, a kidnapper looking for quick money, an extortionist. I can't be distracted. I need to protect you. So, everything personal has to be off-limits."

She said, "Fantastic," but she didn't sound like she meant it.

He shook his head. "I can't be noticing how beautiful you are when I should be watching your surroundings. I can't be laughing with you when anyone around us could be a threat. I can't be silly with happiness and forget who you are, what you represent, how many people want a piece of what you're inheriting. Even if it means hurting you. Some people will stop at nothing to get to you."

She studied him. "I think you see problems where there are none."

"And I think you've led such a quiet life that you forget who you are. But I know who you are, what's at stake. And I will do my job."

She held his gaze for a good minute, but finally shook her head. "All right. I understand."

"Do you?"

She sucked in a breath. "Yes. I'm not sure I'm a hundred percent in agreement. But I can see that's what you believe. So, I respect it."

She turned to leave, and he almost collapsed with relief that he'd won—

Won?

Really? He was going to call it a win that he'd never get to touch her again. Never get to feel the length of her body beneath his.

He cursed. How the hell could he be conflicted when he knew the stakes? She was an incredibly wealthy woman. Even if she refused the estate money, predators would come out of the woodwork. And from here on out if he were to talk about anything personal with her, *that* was what he should be telling her.

That was what he had a responsibility to tell her.

Because for the first time in his life he was genuinely afraid for one of his clients. The estate had been reasonably quiet. Danny was keeping the frauds and fakes in line. But there were a million what-ifs. And if she returned to Pittsburgh alone, opting out of the estate, she'd be a sitting duck.

He shouldn't be teaching her defensive moves.

He shouldn't be telling her he was divorced and had been burned by a client he'd slept with.

He *should* be telling her she needed him—him and his entire staff—to watch her world so no one hurt her.

Just the thought of her alone, even in Pittsburgh, at her jobsite, in her beautiful house, scared him silly. Because she didn't understand the stakes or the risks. And she didn't seem to believe him when he told her.

She headed down the hall to her bedroom. "I think I'll call Leni, see if she wants to go shopping with us. She'd mentioned a boutique where some woman named Iris is very helpful. And my mother loves to shop. This will be a great way to introduce her to Leni, if she's free."

Jace said, "Okay. Sounds good."

She turned and gave him a weak smile. "Yeah. It's super."

She walked away, disappointment shimmering from her, but whether she knew it or not, their world was righting itself.

She needed him.

Especially if her father hadn't died the day his fishing boat caught fire so far out in the ocean everyone *believed* his life raft had drifted into the vast open sea never to be found. *Believed* being the operative word. Without a body how could anyone know for sure?

Jace cursed. Told himself that was nonsense. Crazy thoughts. The ruminations of a guy who overthought everything. Was suspicious of everything. Mark's disappearance had been investigated by professionals.

He could not be alive.

But Jace also knew why the thought had popped into his head. It was better to ponder something ridiculous than endure the upset of knowing he'd hurt Charlotte.

By the time Leni arrived, Charlotte's mom was already at Jace's condo. Penny Fillion walked with Charlotte to the door when Leni's bodyguard opened it.

Charlotte made the round of introductions and her mom stared at Leni. "You are not what I expected."

Her petite half sister smiled as she tucked a strand of her long brown hair behind her ear. "I'm guessing my biological mom was really short."

The three women laughed. Jace did not. He was back to only being her bodyguard.

Disappointment and confusion rippled through Charlotte. Sleeping with Jace was supposed to have been a declaration of independence of a sort. She'd forced herself not to think about a future with him, not to worry that he'd leave her the way her dad had left her mom. At first, it had been terrifying, but she'd stayed in the moment, enjoyed every second, being herself, not feeling the fear, and it had been magnificent.

He had perfect muscles, perfect form and stamina the likes of which she'd never seen. Just thinking about him hovering over her made her want to fan herself.

God, she liked him. She really liked him. But he took his job seriously—and he'd had some bad experiences.

She had, too. Not with other lovers or romantic relationships. With her parents. She should want to be as cautious as he was. After all, this relationship was not going to end in happily-ever-after.

So maybe one night was all she needed? The first step toward overcoming her fears and stepping into the real world.

Maybe, now that she understood what had been happening, why she'd frozen with fear, jumped to conclusions, kicked every guy she'd ever dated to the curb, she really would find "The One."

The three women and two bodyguards rode down in the elevator. They piled into the back of the limo with the chitchat of Charlotte's mom and Leni filling the air. The three women sat on the bench seat facing front. Leni's bodyguard sat with the driver. Jace sat on the seat across from Charlotte, Penny and Leni.

Her mom kept the elevator conversation going, talking about Charlotte's childhood, comparing it to Leni's.

Charlotte sneaked a peek at Jace. He looked out the window, but not like a tourist or someone staring because of boredom. He was truly watching the traffic, watching the street outside the limo when they stopped at a light.

He was so gorgeous, so kind to the people he guarded, that it was hard to imagine a woman hurting him. She must have been a piece of work—

Which was exactly the problem. His marriage had ended in the worst possible way. If that hadn't caused him to never trust again, having a client write a tell-all book had probably sealed the deal.

But she wasn't looking for forever. She sure wasn't going to write a book. And she didn't want to stop what they'd started the night before. She wanted more. She wanted practice with living in the moment, not expecting something she couldn't have.

She wanted a sizzling hot, ridiculously romantic fling, not a one-night stand.

They pulled up in front of a cluster of first-floor shops in what looked to be a part of the financial district, despite the trees, a deli and a coffee shop—Caffeine Burst—on the first floor of the tall buildings. Leni's bodyguard opened the door. Charlotte, her mom and Leni exited, then Jace. Their little train of people entered the store.

Charlotte could have dwelt on the ridiculousness of it, but when the door of the store opened and she saw the white walls and black woodwork, chandeliers and sophisticated dresses, slacks and blouses on the mannequins, she gasped.

"Oh, my gosh! Have we found heaven?"

Leni slid her arm beneath Charlotte's. "No, but it sure as heck feels like it sometimes."

Charlotte's pretty blonde mom reverently said, "I hope I brought all my credit cards."

Charlotte put her hand on her mom's to prevent

her from getting her wallet. "Put your cards away, Mom. This trip is on my dad."

Penny's forehead wrinkled. "What?"

"I got an allowance for these two weeks I'm being vetted. Danny Manelli couriered bank cards to Jace's condo yesterday afternoon. I can't think of a better way to spend my portion than on pretty clothes we can take back to Pittsburgh with us."

Her mom chuckled. "I would like a new dress for Andi Petrunak's wedding."

Leni said, "And there's a fundraiser ball in Scotland next week. If you're staying, why not come with us?"

Penny pressed her hands to her chest. "A ball in Scotland? I'd go to Scotland?"

Leni laughed. "Sure. It's a beautiful event held in a Scottish castle." She nudged her head toward Jace. "It was his family's idea. They put together the event to benefit the children's wing of their local hospital."

Charlotte glanced at Jace. *His family hosted a fundraiser?*

His expression didn't change.

"He won't say it," Leni whispered. "But I think it's his parents' way of getting him to remember his life is with them...and not always with his clients."

"Ah."

"You should come, too," Leni said. "It's a smallish event, though formal. It would be a great way to introduce you around."

"I'm not supposed to be outed yet," Charlotte reminded her. "I haven't been fully vetted, shown the slides or gotten my DNA results back."

Leni shrugged. "So, I'll simply tell people you're my friend. It'll make it even more comfortable for you. That way, when the news breaks, you won't suddenly be thrust into things. Your toes will already be in the pool."

Though she didn't want to be in the pool at all, Charlotte had figured out she wasn't going to be one of Mark Hinton's kids and be totally uninvolved.

She took a breath. "Okay. That makes sense." Facing her mom, she waved her hand over the racks of dresses. "The sky's the limit. We'll add formal dresses to our list."

Leni clapped with glee as a tall, slender woman came down the stairs, wearing pearls that fell to her waist over a black pantsuit with no shirt under the jacket, exposing the upper swell of her breasts.

"That's Iris. She'll find the right dresses for your mom and you, too."

They spent the next hour exploring the shop, with Iris on a mission to find the perfect cocktail dress and gown for Penny.

After discovering two work dresses and trousers with a matching silk blouse, Charlotte moved to the second floor to browse the evening dresses. Jace followed her. While a pretty girl who looked to be in her twenties—Francine—rounded up gowns for her to try on she peeked over at him.

She could brood over his declaration that they'd only have a one-night stand or sigh over how good-looking he was, except now that he'd told her about his divorce and the tell-all book, she saw a little deeper.

He was careful with his clients, went the extra mile for them, because he understood that life wasn't easy. He'd survived the worst kind of breakup of his marriage and the result of his only other one-night stand with a client that nearly wrecked his business. His clients might not go through the exact same things he did, but they didn't have to. He understood pain, heartbreak, embarrassment, loss.

He was one strong, smart, determined guy.

That's why she couldn't be mad at him for laying down the law this morning. She understood him, too.

The first three dresses Francine brought over were good, but the fourth was a formfitting white gown and Charlotte's heart stuttered. She knew what she'd look like in the gown. She didn't even have to try it on.

She glanced at Jace again. If his family was hosting the charity ball, he'd be going. And not as a bodyguard. As a member of the family hosting it.

Wouldn't it be nice to knock his socks off? Especially at an event where he'd just be himself... not the man assigned to protect her?

She could picture it and for the first time realized how unequal their relationship had been from the beginning. She'd thought their stubborn personalities and bossiness made them the same, but in truth he'd been doing his job.

What would it be like if he were just himself?

Would he be charming, kind, sweet, honest?

What would he be like...what would *they* be like—if they were allowed to flirt, laugh, talk, dance—

Without the worry that she was his client or he had responsibilities, they would probably have the best time of their lives and he'd see beyond the ridiculous excuse that she was his client to the real her, the way she'd been seeing the real him since he'd told her about his divorce and his troubles with the tell-all book.

She and Jace needed that ball where they would both be themselves, so he could see they were a good fit.

She might not want forever. But she was done running from good things because she was afraid of the future. She wanted to live her life without fear, without demands. She wanted the chance to be herself.

With Jace.

Francine's phone pinged. She glanced at it, then said, "Your mom is upstairs with Iris. She wants your opinion on a dress. I'll be happy to take that to the register for you."

Caught in a daydream of possibilities about Jace, Charlotte handed her the white gown. "Third floor, right?"

The young clerk smiled. "Third floor."

She made her way up the stairs. Jace discreetly followed her. She snickered. Oh, he was in for a surprise when they went to that ball in Scotland.

But when she reached the top of the stairs, she forgot all about Jace. Her mother stood on a raised platform, wearing a red dress so stunning Charlotte stopped walking.

She had on shiny silver shoes and Iris or Leni had pinned her hair into a loose updo to mimic what she'd look like at Andi's wedding.

She grinned. "What do you think?"

"I think you're beautiful." She suddenly saw what an up-and-coming rich guy might have seen in her mom, twenty-nine years ago. It flashed through her brain that her mom should have spent her life in boutiques like this, buying pretty clothes, attending fancy parties with her dad—

Except her dad hadn't wanted them.

No, he hadn't wanted *her*.

Her mom had pined for him, chatted about him

for the first ten years of Charlotte's life as if one day he'd pop into their world again, live on the farm with them, be a real husband and father.

The next ten years, her mom stopped wishing out loud, but she hadn't lost the spark of hope in her eyes. The past few years, the spark had been gone.

Her mother had literally wasted her life over a man who hadn't wanted her.

She glanced at Jace, Not moving. Looking like a statue.

Her heart swelled in her chest. She felt what her mother must have felt all those years ago. That weird hope. The ridiculous hope that someday he'd see she was what he needed, the woman he wanted—

The night before she'd thought she was declaring her independence, being bold, striking out on her own. But she really liked Jace. Deep down she wanted their relationship to be more than a fling.

Last night, that subconscious expectation had been okay. This morning? Knowing he'd been married and his wife had cheated?

It was wrong.

If there had been one thing her mom had taught her, without words, without actual lessons, it had been that no smart woman ever longed for a man who didn't want her.

No matter how good-looking.

No matter how kind.

No matter how sexy, how gorgeous, how wonderful he was in bed, a smart woman did not get involved with a man who flat out told her he didn't want her.

Not when she really liked him.

Not if she was only kidding herself thinking she could keep anything between them casual.

CHAPTER ELEVEN

THE LIMO DROPPED Leni and her bodyguard at Nick's Park Avenue penthouse. Her cute, sprite-like sister all but skipped into the fancy building.

"She wasn't always like that."

Both Charlotte and her mom looked at Jace. The man hadn't spoken in hours, but suddenly he'd found his voice.

Charlotte glanced back to the building doors closing behind Leni and said, "You mean happy?"

"I mean comfortable with the estate, the money. She didn't merely learn to live with it. She found a way to use it. To make the world a better place."

"Are you hinting that's what I should do?"

He shifted on his seat. "Just reminding you of options. You had fun with her today. She likes you. You like her. You are family now. You should bond."

"Well, look at you going all pop psychologist on us."

"Don't be snarky. This is serious."

"Serious enough for you to break your code

of silence…" She faltered, suddenly recognizing what he was doing. He was treating her like a client. He might not have to tell her to put on pants as he had with Seth Simon, but he was clearly guiding her.

Insult flared inside her until she remembered that he ran a huge security firm that needed the business of Mark Hinton's estate. And that he didn't want her romantically. He'd chosen his company over her, after less than a week of knowing each other, after a night of making love.

She tried not to be insulted. She worked not to think she'd done something wrong. She knew she hadn't. Their night together had been perfect.

But he was choosing his job.

The irony of it was, the first time she'd let herself go out on a limb, do what she wanted, forget her fear of being dumped the way her mom had been…she picked a guy just like her father. A man who chose his job, his work, over her, the way Mark Hinton had with her mother.

Her mom spoke into the silence of the limo. "Your dad would have wanted you and Leni to be friends."

She snorted. "My dad obviously kept us apart for *decades*."

"Maybe he regretted that?"

She gaped at unexpectedly chatty Jace, remembering he'd been close to her dad.

"He told you that?"

"Yeah, he did. Actually, he regretted a couple of things." Jace's gaze slid to her mom and his eyebrows rose.

Oblivious, Penny said, "I think my hotel's right in Times Square."

Charlotte and Jace's gazes bounced to her.

Charlotte said, "Hotel? Aren't you staying with us?"

Jace added, "There's plenty of room in my condo."

Penny laughed and shook her head. "Oh, no, thank you, Jace. I need my space."

Charlotte squeezed her eyes shut. "Don't argue. I spent my childhood on twenty-five acres with the nearest neighbor being a mile away. When she says she likes her space, she means it."

After Jace informed the driver, Charlotte grew angrier and angrier as they drove to her mom's hotel. Jace knew something about Mark Hinton's feelings for her mom. He knew why Mark had kept her and her siblings apart.

They found Penny's hotel, got her checked in and settled in her quiet, comfortable suite and headed back to Jace's condo with Charlotte fuming.

She decided it was a joke of the universe that she should be stuck with a million questions about her dad and the bodyguard who knew him better than anyone. She didn't *want* to have questions about Mark Hinton. She didn't *want* to know about him, didn't *want* to empathize or sympathize. She liked hating him. It put that part of her life into a manageable box. Especially since she didn't need her dad or his money. She was a vice president. Self-sufficient. Independent.

Still...

She'd always wondered if her dad had disliked the idea of being a parent so much that he'd abandoned the love of his life. She'd wondered what would have happened if Penny hadn't gotten pregnant... Would they have been together when Mark died?

And Jace knew.

It gnawed on her brain the rest of the limo ride, in the elevator and as she stormed to her room to—

She didn't know what. They'd had lunch but shopping in one overstocked boutique had taken hours, so it could be time for dinner. She'd laughed with Leni and her mom, feeling like a part of a clique of girls. Two sisters and a mom. And it had been fun.

So fun that she wanted to shake the man silly who'd kept her from it. But he wasn't around. He'd never be around. Sailing off into the afterlife, he avoided all the repercussions of his decisions. But one of his friends was right down the hall. And the temptation to get answers, wrong as it was, overwhelmed her.

She raced from her bedroom, down the hall to the master suite, and punched open the door.

"How dare you tell me things that make me think about my dad! He didn't want me. He didn't want my mom. He kept me from Leni! All this might seem trivial to you, but it wasn't trivial to a little girl being raised away from people because apparently my dad had insisted on that. It wasn't trivial to a little girl who longed for a sister! It wasn't trivial to a mom who'd cried herself to sleep every night for at least ten years! I managed to get myself beyond the questions. Beyond caring. And a few comments from you has me curious about him. So damned curious because the way the math lines up, he left my mom when she got pregnant. Which means *I* was the catalyst for him leaving!"

She stopped. Her lungs pooled with air so heavy it made her eyes tingle, then fill with tears.

"You were but not for the reasons you think. Your dad knew his being around you, living with you, even marrying your mom, put you in danger."

"So, you're sticking with his story that he was protecting us."

"He was!" Jace sighed. "Charlotte, having tons of money wasn't just the issue. He did some wheeling and dealing and not always in the nicest possible way. He made enemies in the '80s. Lots of enemies. Some of them were mobbed up. Some of them were connected to cartels. Most of them are dead now, but when your mom got pregnant, he was getting a death threat every week. He really believed hiding you was the best thing."

"Don't make excuses for him deserting us!" She plopped down onto the bed. "Don't you see? No matter how you slice this, my mom and I were alone. If one of his enemies had found us, we would have been helpless. What you just told me makes it even worse that he deserted us!" She sucked in a breath as tears fell. "How is that the best thing?"

Jace's chest froze. He'd never seen her so vulnerable. He'd never seen anyone so vulnerable. The raw pain in her eyes tore at him, ravaged his soul. He realized it was the same kind of pain he'd felt when his wife cheated with his best friend. Raw, broken, he'd lashed out when he simply wanted... no, *needed*...someone to explain. No one could.

He couldn't stand back and watch her struggle. Not when he knew the pain was different, worse, than anything she'd ever felt.

He sat beside her on the bed, wrapped his arm around her and pulled her close. "I'm sorry. I'll keep my mouth shut from here on."

She shoved back. "I'm not sure I want that, either. It's like I'm finding things out that hurt but I need to know them. I feel like I have to know... like I'm on the edge of something."

"You are. You're on the edge of a new life. A

whole new life as a wealthy woman who can do anything she wants."

He thought that would soothe her, but her eyes filled with tears again.

"Leni and I could have been best friends."

"You still can."

She nodded, looking as if she was hitting the place of acceptance, but he saw a softness in her face that made his heart hurt and his limbs weak. The instinct that it was his job to comfort her morphed into something more. An ache to love her, to soothe her by showing her how special she was.

He told himself not to kiss her. He moved closer, anyway. How could he resist her when she needed comfort, needed to know that she mattered? His mouth drifted over hers in a touch as light as a hummingbird's wings. But that only fueled the fire of desire, igniting his own need. His lips pressed. She responded by opening hers to him, and almost in a trance of yearning, he deepened the kiss. Keeping his wits but allowing himself the simple pleasure that would calm her wounded soul.

She wrapped her arms around his neck, and he let her melt into him. Degree by degree, what began as comfort shifted into something sweet, but scorching.

She'd worn a simple T-shirt and jeans to meet Leni, and as his hand drifted over the soft material, the longing to feel the velvety skin beneath it raced through him like a brushfire.

And why shouldn't he? This relationship was a nonstarter. After their talk this morning, they both knew it. Neither one of them would get ideas of forever.

But they also both felt something incomprehensible in each other's arms. They'd found a unique peace the night before. He genuinely believed she needed to feel that again. To get the comfort or the grounding or maybe simply a night away from the stress, the worry, of everything her life was about to become.

Still kissing her, he slid his fingers under the hem of her T-shirt and lifted it over her head. They pulled apart to accommodate the shirt, and when he popped it off, their gazes met.

He answered the curiosity in her eyes by leaning in to kiss her, softly, slowly. This was no ordinary woman, no ordinary act. Had he met her before Mary Beth, Charlotte might have been the love of his life.

No. She was definitely the love of his life. So, he made love to her that way. With a respect that manifested his simple awe. Awe that she was so smart, so beautiful and, for at least the next few hours, *his*.

The word turned over in his head, flicked a switch of something purely male inside him. Possessiveness merged with the hormones currently ruling his brain and caused him to take greedily.

But she surprised him, pushing him down on the bed and standing long enough to remove her jeans. Realizing what a great idea that was, he rid himself of his clothes, and when she crawled on the bed to straddle him, they were naked. Flesh to flesh, the way he truly believed they were supposed to be.

The rest happened in a blur. One minute she was in control, the next he wrestled it away from her. He might have considered it a competition, except he loved her strength, fed off her power over him until a tidal wave of release rumbled through them both, stealing his breath and hers.

He squeezed his eyes shut, allowed himself one quick burst of anger that fate would bring her into his life when he couldn't have her, then he rolled them together on the bed. She snuggled against him and sighed with contentment but didn't speak. For which he was grateful. He wanted the next five minutes to simply enjoy the feel of her.

But his thoughts wouldn't give him the luxury of peace. They crowded him, mocked him. Though he'd gotten past the worry that she was a client, he couldn't stop the knowledge that she was a woman on the edge of an enormous life, the likes of which she couldn't even imagine.

He'd thought making love to her would help her relax enough to come to terms with some of it…

But he hadn't expected to have feelings again.

Or to want something he couldn't have.

He wasn't good at things like intimacy or relationships. But he could keep people safe. And Charlotte, brave, strong, honest-to-a-fault Charlotte, needed a relationship. Someone to show her the love she'd been denied—

He could not be that man.

There was no easy answer, so he let himself fall asleep with her in his arms.

CHAPTER TWELVE

CHARLOTTE'S PACKAGES WERE sitting on the kitchen island with the doorman's card tidily attached to the top of one of the boxes. Jace had fallen asleep and she'd had to carefully slide out of bed to keep from waking him. She might be hungry, but she knew exhaustion when she saw it, so she let him sleep and found her way to the kitchen.

She grabbed her purchases and hung them in her closet. She stopped when she came to the expensive shimmery white gown. Not taken off the rack, but something pulled from a private showroom. Something special. Something unique.

Almost a physical symbol of her segue from one kind of life into another.

She'd gone to Jace's room to confront him. Instead, he'd comforted her. There'd be repercussions. He had probably mentally lambasted himself for allowing himself to make love again.

But she didn't regret it. Not one bit. This time she'd kept the thought in her head that he didn't want her forever and she didn't want him forever.

But she did want what they had. They couldn't help getting close. They were together all day, every day. He saw everything going on in her life. And she genuinely believed fate had tossed them together to show her that she could be involved in a temporary relationship and not die, or wither, or fall into a deep depression, when it ended.

Because it would end. He was divorced. His wife had cheated. That kind of wound left scars. And she wasn't arrogant enough to think she could heal them.

She made a ham sandwich and grabbed a bottle of water from the refrigerator and walked to the TV room.

So, they had what they had.

And what if that was what life was all about?

Accepting the good things that came your way and not expecting perfection.

She thought about how she'd always searched for "The One," and shook her head. Maybe it was time to get rid of that notion, too.

She heard noises outside the TV room and knew Jace was awake. She wouldn't run out to the kitchen, scramble after him like a lovesick pup. Charlotte wasn't a chaser, and she didn't think Jace was the kind of guy who liked to be chased. This was about a mutual attraction. They could fight something that felt as natural as breathing or enjoy it.

She chose to enjoy it.

The question was…would he?

"I see you don't need dinner."

She turned to the door. He looked rumpled and well loved. If she were a woman predisposed to pride, she would have grinned. "I eat a lot of sandwiches in my world."

He ambled into the room and plopped on the sofa beside her. As he slid one arm around her, he picked up the television remote with the other and turned on the Yankees baseball game, muting the sound.

"Are you a fan?"

"Half the population of the United States are fans."

She shrugged. "I like the Pittsburgh Pirates."

He laughed. "Then you're loyal."

Funny that he should mention loyalty since that seemed to be the one trait he valued most. "They have their years."

"Not many." He glanced at her from his peripheral vision. "Which makes your loyalty extremely rare."

"What can I say? I'm special that way." And she suddenly sensed they weren't talking about baseball anymore.

"Loyalty is a good trait."

"It's an essential trait. It's the kind of trait that keeps a lover from writing a tell-all book."

He laughed.

She snuggled closer, though she reminded herself she wasn't going to push him into continuing their affair. She would let it be his choice.

"This is nice."

Her heart lifted a bit, but an icy fear filled her chest. She might not want forever but she hated leaving it all up to chance. She at least wanted him to say what they had could continue. "Yeah. It is."

"You know, we can't pretend that we fell into bed this afternoon. I had a few chances to back out. So did you. We also can't pretend that won't happen again."

The iceberg in her chest melted a bit. He wasn't telling her they had to stop. Maybe he'd figured out some things about them, too?

"Nope. No such pretending will be done by me."

"We can't pretend I won't do this when we're alone." He drew her forward and kissed her thoroughly.

She smiled at him as he pulled away. The kiss had been hot enough to totally melt her iceberg of fear. "I think I like where this conversation is going."

"Every minute I'm with you, I want to talk, I want to touch, I want to kiss you."

"I really like where this conversation is going."

"Yeah, well. You don't know everything about me."

"There's more than a divorce and crappy affair?"

* * *

Jace took a quiet breath. Common sense precluded him from even trying to pretend they wouldn't sleep together again, but he also couldn't go on with what was happening between them unless he was sure she understood this wouldn't lead anywhere.

And not just because he couldn't trust. Because he didn't want to hurt her.

"That's the worst of it."

She frowned. "So, what you would be springing on me now are bad habits and goofy things you did in high school?"

He shook his head, feeling clumsy and out of his element. A man accustomed to one-night stands, he usually didn't have to talk about his feelings. "Probably. I guess what I'm trying to say is I love what we have. I don't want it to end, but it's going to."

"Okay."

He sighed. She was not cutting him any slack. She was going to make him say it. "But if we're both on the same page, there's no reason we can't continue."

"What about your bodyguard duties?"

He wouldn't tell her that getting so close to her would make him crazy vigilant. He hadn't yet worked out if that was good or bad.

"Aren't you the one who said that getting involved made you think my bossiness was sexy?"

She laughed. "Yes."

"You paying attention to me is fifty percent of the battle when I guard you. We'll work as a team and everything will be fine."

"I still say I'm not in any danger and you see a witch under every wisteria."

He shook his head. "Whatever." Having said his piece and content they were in agreement, he distracted her by sliding his hand to her nape and under her glorious hair. "Did you get something to wear to the ball in Scotland?"

"Yes. I did. And I think you're going to love it."

He probably would. He loved everything she did.

When he didn't answer right away, her eyes clouded. "You are going to the ball, aren't you?"

"Are you kidding? This is my grandmother's baby. She'd skin me alive if I tried to skip out."

Her face brightened. "So, you won't be going as a bodyguard?"

"I'm visiting my family, going to a fundraiser they host. Plus, Scotland is a fairly safe place for you and Leni. No one cares about the Hinton heirs there. I'll bet if we asked people on the street in Scotland nobody would even know there were Hinton heirs. Actually, while we're there, pretending we're dating would keep me close enough to do my job, and maybe we could have some fun."

Her face contorted. A smart woman, she never took anything at face value. "So, you're pretending it's okay for you to like me so that when we go to Scotland it will be a great way to guard me?"

"No. I'm saying going to Scotland is a perk. A bonus." He met her gaze. "I can't pretend I don't like you."

Her eyes grew soft and dewy. "I can't pretend I don't like you, either. It seems a shame that our lives are eventually going to force us apart."

"Yeah, but we have right now." He drew her close, kissed her. That was another thing he loved about her. Her logic. He broke the kiss and whispered in her ear, "Let's go back to bed and see what happens."

She laughed. He rose, took her hand and led her to his master suite.

They woke together the next morning. She gave him a sleepy smile and that was all his hormones needed. After slow, easy lovemaking they showered together and laughed as she tried to wear a pair of his sweatpants and a T-shirt so they could go to the kitchen to get breakfast.

"I have a better idea. Let's go out to eat."

"You're letting me out among people?"

"You were out with people yesterday."

"Yeah, right. Iris kept us hidden."

He laughed. "It's why we love her. But I was thinking we should do something fun like take your mom to Junior's. It's a restaurant in Times Square. Near her hotel and she will love it."

Her eyes widened. "Seriously?"

"Sure. Put on your best jeans and get ready for heaven. Their cheesecake is to die for."

"So, we're not just going out for breakfast? We're going to be bad and eat cheesecake for breakfast?"

"Oh, honey, we passed bad a long time ago."

She snickered. "Yeah, we did."

"Call your mom and tell her to be ready in forty minutes. I'll touch base with Nick and arrange for you to see some of the slides this afternoon."

She turned to head back to her bedroom to dress. "Sounds like a plan."

Charlotte's mom glowed like a lamp. Happy to be out with her daughter, she chatted the whole time they were at Junior's. Charlotte was thrilled to see her so bubbly. The cheesecake was a wonderful, decadent breakfast and Charlotte felt like she was floating.

In his T-shirt and jeans, with a black leather jacket, Jace looked like sex on a spoon. She saw women giving him sideways glances and some even sighing.

She wanted to say, "Hey, eyes on your own paper," as happy possessiveness overwhelmed her. Except he wasn't really hers. They both understood that once she'd seen the slides of what her dad owned and her DNA results came back, decisions would have to be made, but sheesh.

Look at him. All gorgeous and manly, drinking his coffee and polishing off his cheesecake. She'd known this relationship wouldn't last forever, but sometimes, like right now…she wished it would… wished it *could*.

But neither one of them could promise tomorrow. Charlotte was finally beginning to understand she had no idea what would happen in her future. Whether she took the money or not, her life would change.

As they rose from the table, she said, "You know, Mom, you could come to Nick and Leni's with us to see the slides of things my father owned."

Her mom kept her attention on her purse as she pulled it from the back of her chair and slid the strap up her arm.

"Maybe another time." She glanced around, taking a long breath. "I feel like sightseeing."

Jace went for his phone. "I'll get you a driver."

Penny stopped him by putting her hand on his before it reached his pocket. "I want to walk."

"It would still be better if you had someone with you."

Penny smiled. "Maybe yes. Maybe no."

Jace scowled.

Realizing how much she'd love the opportunity to explore on her own, Charlotte said, "She's fine."

"You're damned right I'm fine." Penny laughed. "No one cares about a woman who looks like an average tourist." Heading out of the restaurant, she slid on her sunglasses. "Besides I have mace."

She walked up the street, away from them, toward the M&M store, and Charlotte laughed.

"She'll be fine."

Jace got his phone. "I'm having someone follow her, anyway."

She shook her head. "Just can't leave bodyguard mode, can you?"

"If you saw an iffy spot in the blueprints for one of your company's buildings, would you walk away without mentioning it?"

She sighed. "No."

"Okay, then."

Deciding to forget about his job and just enjoy the day, she shook her head. "You know. It might be fun for *us* to do a few touristy things." She inched closer, linked her arm with his. "See a Broadway play. Have dinner somewhere fancy." She peeked at him. "You know, since we figured out that pretending to date makes it less obvious that I have a bodyguard."

"It does work."

She grinned. "Let's go get tickets."

In the limo driving to Nick's, Jace went online and bought tickets for a show that evening.

They entered Nick's condo to find Leni in the kitchen, wearing an apron.

"I'm making cookies," she called to them as they stepped inside and removed their coats.

Nick took their jackets to a nearby closet. "I love cookies."

Leni came over and gave Nick a quick, smacking kiss. "It was a batch of Christmas cookies that won him over."

Charlotte laughed. "I know there's a story in there somewhere."

"A good one actually." The stove timer pinged, and Leni raced back to the kitchen area. Calling over her shoulder, she said, "But you're going to need days to see all these slides, so we'll save that discussion for another time."

They walked to a back room where Nick had pulled the drapes closed and synced his computer with a huge television. The picture of a white stone mansion filled the screen.

Nick sat on the chair by the computer. "That's your dad's primary residence. A mansion in Ohio."

Charlotte slowly lowered herself to the sofa. Jace leaned against the doorjamb watching. The first few slides showed the rooms of the house, and her mouth fell open slightly.

The place dripped with luxury.

The next house was equally gorgeous. A huge cabin in Denver. The next house was in Aspen.

"Why two houses in Colorado?"

"Well, Aspen's an hour drive from Denver and your dad liked to ski."

"Oh. Okay." She sat back and got comfortable.

By the time they got up to his seventeenth house, Charlotte's brain was mush.

"Did he even remember he had all these houses?"

Nick laughed. "No. That's part of my company's duties for him. We don't just manage his money. We keep track of his *things*." He flicked to the next slide. "Now, we start on beach houses."

The four Jace had mentioned the night she'd met Nick and Leni were first. Then two smaller lake houses came on the screen.

Then a spotless little house on an island.

Seeing the tiny, inconspicuous house, Jace pushed away from the wall. His mouth fell open. His eyes narrowed. His breath stalled.

Damn it!

That house might not be beside the scene of Mark's boating accident, but it was close enough Mark could have gotten there if he got his lifeboat to shore.

He didn't even bother to excuse himself. He opened the door and left the room. Racing to the main living area of the condo, Jace looked for Leni. When he found her in the kitchen, he said, "Is there someplace private that I could use to make a call?"

"Nick's office." She led him down the hall and opened a door on a compact space. "There's a desk and chair, even a computer if you need it."

"Thanks."

She said, "You're welcome," closing the door behind her as she left him alone.

So angry he could barely speak, Jace checked for listening devices and cameras. When he found nothing, he pulled out his cell phone and dialed the number for Mark's international phone.

He let it ring fourteen times. It didn't go to voice mail, simply disconnected, so he called again. Again, it rang fourteen times, then disconnected.

He scrubbed his hand across his mouth. Not sure if he should feel foolish for his suspicion or relieved that no one had answered Mark's phone, he wasn't quite ready to go back to the room with Charlotte. Instead, he touched base with his supervisors, put out a few fires, then returned to the media room where Charlotte and Nick were still watching slides.

The sight of Mark Hinton's properties and possessions gave Jace an odd feeling. Sadness poured through him as he remembered being with Mark in his cars or riding on Jet Skis. He suddenly wondered if his suspicion wasn't simply a part of grief. The denial part. Maybe thinking Mark had faked his death was easier than the reality that he'd never see his friend again.

Out of sorts and not in the mood to look at slides of houses and cars and eight tons of furniture, he walked to the kitchen where Leni was putting white icing on sugar cookies. Little bottles of red, blue and yellow sprinkles sat at the ready, waiting to add color.

Leni handed him one. "You look like you could use something sweet."

He wasn't sure what he needed, but he took the cookie, bit into it and groaned. "So good."

"I love to bake," she said, smiling as she iced another cookie. "My mom taught me."

"Well, she did a good job."

"Hey." Charlotte entered the kitchen. "Oh! Cookies are done!"

Laughing, Leni handed her one. "All finished with day one of the slides?"

Charlotte rolled her eyes. "Two hours was all I could take."

Icing cookies, Leni said, "That's why the estate allows a few days to look at everything."

"I can hardly wait to get to the Ming vases. How can one person keep track of so much crap?"

Jace reached for another cookie. "He couldn't. That's why Nick keeps the lists and the slides."

Charlotte sighed. "So he said."

Nick brought their jackets. "So, I guess you'll be back tomorrow?"

"Only if I can't think of a good excuse to bow out."

Nick laughed. "I know. It's boring. But your dad's will insists that you see all the slides."

Jace laughed, but he also remembered how desperately Mark had wanted his kids to be introduced to his life, his lifestyle.

Putting it into his will that his kids had to look at all the slides suddenly seemed very convenient.

He stomped out his suspicions. He was grieving Mark. That was all this was. Denial. He was going to have to get to the point of acceptance soon or he'd say or do something that would make everyone think he was crazy.

Or make Charlotte run away. She already believed her dad was a mean-spirited con man. If she discovered Jace was having these weird suspicions, she'd be furious.

CHAPTER THIRTEEN

THE WEEK PASSED quickly for Charlotte. The Broadway play she and Jace saw was funny. Dinner afterward was romantic. She spent most mornings with Nick, looking at slides, but in the afternoon, she shopped with her mom, who loved being in New York. She had a glow about her that Charlotte had never seen. But she still liked her private time. Stayed in the hotel. Noticed the bodyguard Jace had assigned to her, and when she couldn't lose him, she sent him home.

Which made Charlotte laugh. Pretending to be dating, she and Jace had gone out like a couple, returned to his condo to sleep together and brought each other coffee every morning, depending on who woke first.

It was the perfect week. So, the evening they left for Scotland, on Jace's big plane, with Nick and Leni to arrive the next day in his jet, it seemed odd to Charlotte that Jace was uncharacteristically nervous.

"I'm the one who doesn't like takeoffs and

landings," she reminded him, plopping down on the seat she'd been in the first time they'd flown. Though she had a carry-on with pajamas for sleeping through the long flight, her luggage had been taken by the driver in their condo and she'd comfortably accepted that she wouldn't see it again until they got to Jace's grandmother's home.

Noting that her mother was busy exploring the plane, she said, "Why are you nervous?"

Jace shook his head at her. "You and I have more or less agreed this is a short-term thing between us—"

She'd argue that. Whatever was between them was strong. And though it might not last forever, she sincerely doubted it was short-term.

Still, a good poker player didn't show her hand. She played it. She trusted her gut that she'd know when to quit. Until then she planned to make the most of every minute they had together.

"And I'm about to introduce you to my family."

She laughed. "You're afraid that after they meet me and see what a great person I am, they'll trounce you when you dump me."

He sat beside her. When he caught her gaze, his eyes were oddly serious. "What makes you think I'll dump you? What if you dump me?"

"Then you'll get their sympathy. Because I am quite a catch."

He snorted.

The plane taxied to the runway and Jace took her hand. "Not gonna kiss me this time, are you?"

She glanced back at her mom, who had her nose in a book. "Let's see how it goes."

His brow furrowed. "You don't want to kiss me in front of your mom?"

"I don't think I've ever kissed a man in front of my mom."

"There's a first time for everything…"

But the private plane had already found the runway and was shooting into the sky. Charlotte's heart skipped a beat. Her chest tightened to the point that she wasn't sure she could breathe, and she began counting in her head to distract herself.

Then it was over. They were airborne.

"You're beginning to get beyond your fear."

She relaxed. He had no idea how many fears she'd been conquering with him. "I think I am."

"If you participate in the estate, you'll fly like this all the time and pretty soon you'll grow so accustomed to takeoffs and landings they'll be nothing for you."

It was the first he'd mentioned the estate in days and she almost hated that he had. The real test of their relationship would be if she took her share of the money. Figuring out what to do with it, she'd enter a new phase of her life. She guessed that would require travel, meeting people, investigating charities…

Jace could still be her bodyguard but that seemed tacky. She'd be the cliché heiress sleeping with her bodyguard. If she had to have someone following her around, it would be better for it to be a neutral party.

But then she and Jace would never see each other.

She tried to think that through but there were no easy answers. He was busy. She would be, too. And if she decided not to take her share of the money, she'd go back to Pittsburgh. Unless he found time to make a special trip to her city—or if she flew to New York—their time together would be over.

Either way, her acceptance or refusal of her dad's money would end them.

Not wanting to think about that anymore, she unbuckled her seat belt and walked to the back of the jet to get the cards. She suggested to her mom that a good start to the flight would be a few games of rummy before they hunkered down and got some sleep.

Her mom closed her book. "I'd like that. We haven't played rummy since you built that fancy house of yours."

"Then come on over to the table."

They played cards for two hours before her mom yawned. A gentleman, Jace gave the bedroom to Charlotte and Penny. As he settled into one of the reclining seats to sleep, she and her mom went to the back of the plane to the little room with the big bed.

Behind the closed door, her mom said, "You like him."

"A lot. But cool your jets. The man was burned by a really bad marriage."

Penny slid into her pajamas. "Aww. You don't think it's going to last."

"Actually, we've agreed that it's not going to last."

"Oh, no." Her mom's face saddened. "I see what's happening. You're protecting yourself because of what happened with your dad."

"No!" But she had been. Jace was the first guy with whom she wasn't protecting herself. The first time she was letting nature take its course, and not worrying about the inevitable ending.

Her mom sighed. "Not every relationship ends in goodbye and even the ones that do are sometimes worth the trouble. Worth the memories. Worth the good times."

Charlotte shook her head. That had been her rationale about sleeping with Jace. Which she did not want to discuss with her mom.

Penny sat on the bed, tucked her legs beneath her. "I remember meeting your dad." She sighed. "He was so tall and so good-looking. Our first date he took me to Italy for spaghetti." She laughed and shook her head. "The first time we slept together he took me to Paris for breakfast. We ice skated, fished, rode horses, skied in Switzerland. The three years we were together he made my life rich. Fun. But also important. He needed me. He said I grounded him, gave him strength. He also said losing me was the hardest thing he'd ever endured."

Seeing the love in her mom's eyes, Charlotte's eyes filled with tears. "You never told me any of this stuff before."

Penny inclined her head. "I wasn't about to tell my ten-year-old daughter intimate details about her mom and dad."

"True. But you could have told me about Italy and the spaghetti. When I got older you could have told me some of the other stuff."

"And you would have liked hearing those things about him?"

Charlotte winced. "I don't know."

"I do," Penny said firmly. "You hated your dad. Didn't want to hear his good points." She smiled. "And he really did have his good points. Like he was funny. And generous. Unfortunately, he was also ruthless when it came to a business deal."

Charlotte pulled in a breath for the first time in her life picturing her dad making a deal, being sharp, being determined—

A little too much like herself for Charlotte's comfort.

"Well, he certainly had to have been a good businessman to amass his fortune."

Penny smiled. "You're a lot like him that way."

She squeezed her eyes shut, not wanting the comparison, but it wasn't as revolting as it might have been. Since getting involved with Jace she hadn't just sloughed off her own fears, she'd begun understanding her mother's love for Mark.

Though Charlotte wouldn't wait almost thirty years for a man, she could understand the love her mother had felt for the reclusive billionaire.

"I'm starting to see you thought he was pretty special."

"He was." She laughed. "But he was a bit crazy, too. Paranoid, yet somehow easygoing. Ruthless but generous." Penny crawled to the head of the bed and pulled back the covers. "Everybody's complicated, Charlotte."

"I hadn't thought I was until this week."

Her mom peeked up at her. "What happened?"

She slid under the blankets of the queen-size bed and plopped onto the pillow. She wasn't about to tell her mom that she'd just figured out she dumped every guy she'd dated because she didn't want to get hurt the way her mom had. Penny deserved the good memories she had of Mark Hinton. She'd certainly earned them with over twenty-eight years of devotion.

"Meeting Leni, thinking about being an heiress." She laughed. "That one's like a punch in the gut."

"You could do so much good with that money."

"Probably. But now's not the time to think about it. We're lucky to have a long enough flight to get some sleep because it will be morning in Scotland when we get there."

She closed her eyes, indicating to her mom that she was too sleepy to keep talking, but her mind rolled on and on. She thought about how lucky Mark had been to have her mom and it warmed her heart. Her mother never disputed that her dad was a tad crazy, but she'd loved him because he needed someone to love him.

Maybe like Jace?

She always thought of her life in terms of goals. Meeting Jace she'd learned to live in the moment. Now she had to wonder...

Her mother had sacrificed her entire life for Mark Hinton, raised his child, lived alone.

Jace didn't need her to sacrifice her life, but he did need her unconditional love. Not the love of someone who enjoyed his company but the love of someone who gave him the benefit of the doubt, put his needs before her own...

That was stupid. They were equal. Neither one had to put the other's needs ahead of their own.

Plus continuing what they had didn't work. The man had been burned. He didn't want a relationship.

And she did want a relationship. Someday.

She'd find a nice guy, maybe someone who was also in construction and development, and they'd have a normal courtship and marry under the big oak in her mom's backyard, have kids—

The thought of living her life with anyone other than Jace squeezed her chest, brought tears to her eyes. The display of emotion concerned her more than the thought of living her life without Jace.

She'd worked all this out. Until she'd heard that wonderful softness in her mom's voice. The happiness that made no sense. The emotion that could only be described as real love.

She wanted that real love so bad that her heart hurt, but even as she thought that she pictured Jace. Thought about what they had. Thought about how she felt with him and the heart squeeze that resulted shook her to her core—

Surely, she hadn't fallen in love with Jace in less than two weeks?

She flopped over on her pillow. No. She couldn't. She'd known all along her relationship with Jace was just about fun. She wouldn't even let herself consider the possibility that she'd fallen in love with someone she couldn't have.

But what if she had?

Her mom fell asleep almost immediately. Charlotte slept restlessly. She woke before her mom, checked the time and slipped into jeans and a sweater before going out to the main section of the plane.

Jace slept soundly.

She inched her way to the seat about two feet

away from his, sat on the arm and watched him.
The first nights at her house, he hadn't more than
catnapped. Once they began sleeping together,
he'd eased into deep, restful sleep. As if everything in his world was okay when she was beside him.

Their connection was so strong it was hard to
believe they weren't a happily-ever-after couple.
But they weren't. He did not want to commit, and
she was testing the waters of a casual relationship,
something she'd never done. For once, she wasn't
looking for "The One," wasn't putting that bur-
den on someone.

Except he was so kind, so sexy, so wonderful,
the temptation was strong to believe—

One of his eyes opened. "Am I drooling or
something?"

She laughed and rose from the seat's arm. "No.
But if my calculations are correct, we should be
landing in about half an hour."

He yawned and stretched. "Good. Go wake
your mom."

Her mother woke slowly and grumpily, and
once she was out of bed, Charlotte left her alone
to dress. A few minutes later, Penny sat on the
seat across the aisle from the two seats Jace and
Charlotte were in.

Jace said, "Good morning."

Penny mustered a smile.

Then the plane began to descend. Charlotte

squeezed Jace's hand when the wheels bounced onto the runway, but otherwise she was fine.

Jace gave her a quick, sloppy kiss of praise, and when they realized he'd kissed her in front of her mom, they both laughed. The night before her mom had guessed they'd started something…no point in not kissing. But there was something about coming out, letting other people know they'd started a romance, that almost made her giddy.

She shook her head to clear it. No matter how many people they told, how happy they were together, how sad it would be not to spend the rest of her life with him—it would end. And if she didn't stop longing for things that weren't going to happen, she'd miss the last few days of fun she had with him.

They gathered jackets and carry-ons and headed to the waiting limo. The drive was longer than she expected and by the time they reached the MacDonald family home—which was more of an estate—Charlotte was starving.

A man and woman about the same age as Penny raced out of the main house, a huge stone dwelling that Charlotte could tell was not only at least a hundred years old, it had to have six bedrooms, maybe eight.

"Mom," Jace said as he hugged the dark-haired woman, then the tall man with hair that had begun to gray at the temples.

He faced Charlotte. "Mom and Dad, this is Charlotte Fillion and her mom, Penny."

Charlotte went to shake hands and instead was enveloped in a huge hug first by Jace's mom, then his dad.

A light laugh escaped. "Well, it's nice to meet you, too."

"You can call me Lorraine," Jace's mom said as she looped her arm through Penny's. "And my husband is Bill."

Charlotte nodded, noting the lack of Scottish accent and remembering that Jace's parents lived in the United States. His brother and sister-in-law were living with his aging grandmother, but their home was also in the States.

There was something sweet about the way the whole family clearly considered Scotland and this estate their roots, their home base.

Lorraine led Penny toward the front door. A newish garage built to look like an old-fashioned carriage house was off to the left. Three other structures made a semicircle to the right. A barn sat in the distance. Morning dew covered the lawn. Crisp, clean air filled her nostrils.

Charlotte glanced around. "Reminds me of being ten and taking my breakfast outside so I could gobble it down on the way to the barn to get my bike for a morning ride."

Jace's stomach growled. "Speaking of breakfast." He laughed and put his arm across her shoulders. "Let's go inside."

Charlotte nodded. Little things like that—incidental, wonderful things like the easy way he put his arm around her—sent her mind in that bad direction again. The one where she could see their future. See their lives intersecting and how they could help each other. See their kids. A beach house for weekends.

Craziness. All of it. They'd stated their intentions, and as far as Charlotte was concerned, that was a verbal contract. She wouldn't break it with new demands. No matter how much the squishy feeling in her stomach meshed with the softness in her mom's voice when she talked about Mark Hinton, Charlotte refused to believe she'd fallen in love.

They headed up a cobblestone path to the house, which was lovely. Modern furniture had been supplemented with heavy cupboards and side tables that were clearly antique.

In the kitchen, where a long table had been set for seven, a younger version of Jace and a sunny, dark-haired, clearly pregnant woman stood by the counter, filling platters with eggs, sausage, bacon and toast.

Jace nudged her. "That's my brother, Oliver, and his wife, Emily."

She smiled at the pair as she and Jace sat. "Nice to meet you."

Jace said, "This is Charlotte."

Walking to the table, his brother and sister-in-law both said, "Nice to meet you."

It was odd that no one questioned her presence, or razzed Jace about having a girlfriend, but she suspected Jace had told them not to make a big deal. Which was kind of cute and funny, even as it was sad. They probably thought Jace didn't want to be embarrassed, when the truth was Charlotte would be disappearing from their lives.

After Emily and Oliver sat, Jace's mom started the platter of eggs around the circle of people. His dad picked up the platter of sausage links, snagged three and passed it around.

Charlotte filled her plate.

Jace said, "I thought you didn't like breakfast."

"Maybe it's the air," she said as she reached for toast. "But I'm starving."

Emily said, "It's chilly this morning. That always makes me hungry."

The conversation went on like that naturally and easily. When Charlotte asked about Jace's grandmother, Emily laughed and said, "She sleeps till ten."

That began a lively discussion about the seventy-eight-year-old MacDonald matriarch, who still kept chickens, a cow and a few goats. Even as Charlotte enjoyed the easy camaraderie of family, she also felt the sting of having been raised alone. She now had Leni, but other than that, she only had her mom. Though she would try to see her half sister often—

Actually, if she took her share of the estate, maybe she and Leni could team up, looking for charities and benefits and ways to put their father's money to good use.

It was an excellent plan, but sitting in the country kitchen, enjoying Jace's family, it somehow seemed hollow. She and Leni had missed so much it was hard to believe they could form this kind of solid, easy bond.

When breakfast was finished and everyone was talked out, Lorraine and Bill led their visitors upstairs where their driver had taken their suitcases. The last one on the stairs, Charlotte paused to watch Emily and Oliver work together to gather the dishes and tidy the kitchen.

There was something about the pair that tugged on her heartstrings. Maybe it was because they were expecting their first baby. Maybe it was because they were young and starting out together with nothing but each other.

But something about them got to her. They were so easily in love. So natural with each other. So loving. So committed—

Her head tilted as she studied them. She'd bet her bottom dollar that Emily never wondered if Oliver would commit to her. She'd bet her last cent that Oliver hadn't played hard to get or warned Emily that he would never trust enough to have another relationship. She'd bet everything she had that they'd taken one look at each other, blushed and flirted, and from that moment on, they'd been inseparable.

Nothing like the way she and Jace had sparred and tried to hold back from flirting. Nothing like the way he'd warned her he wouldn't ever commit again, and how they'd settled for what they could get, both too afraid to take a real step—

She shook her head to clear it.

She was not too afraid. Being with Jace was her way of proving she *wasn't* afraid.

She had to stop overthinking this. What she and Jace had was like a verbal agreement and she wasn't allowed to redefine it—

No matter how much she wished she could.

With a groan, she started down the hall to the room she would share with Jace. No one else had a problem with them as a couple. And if she hadn't seen his sister-in-law's pregnant belly and his brother's glowing eyes, she wouldn't, either.

Would she?

Her heart melted in her chest. She'd always wanted kids. Always wanted a home like this one filled with love and camaraderie. No matter how hard she tried to pretend the thought hadn't entered her head, Jace was the guy she kept putting in the picture of her future.

He was strong and smart and sexy and would be a great dad—

She had to stop. She'd begun this relationship knowing it would end. Changing the rules wasn't fair. Not to Jace or herself.

Planning a future that wasn't going to happen was how people got hurt.

The first day of their visit, Jace took Charlotte and her mom to see the sights. His grandmother let Penny feed her chickens, which was equal parts of funny and sweet. Jace didn't think he'd ever laughed so hard at someone doing barnyard chores.

The following morning they lazed around on the back porch, reading and in general relaxing. That afternoon, Lorraine took Penny and Charlotte to a beauty shop in town to get their hair done for the ball. Jace employed the driver of the limo that took them into town and knew neither his mom nor Charlotte would be surprised when he came into the shop and discreetly watched the door.

Though Penny had her hair fancied up in some sort of hairdo that swept her blond locks into looping curls, Charlotte's hair looked as it had the day she'd gone to work to tell her boss she'd be away for a few weeks.

The way Jace liked it.

Memories of that morning trickled through him. Picking up her earring in the elevator, feeling things he hadn't ever felt. Not even with Mary Beth. And now here they were, lovers.

He put on his tux, struggling with the bow tie as she dressed in the bathroom off their bedroom. He heard the door open and automatically turned, the instinct of a bodyguard always taking charge. When she stepped out, wearing the slinky white gown, her curves outlined, her height somehow accented instead of downplayed, his heart stuttered.

"You look amazing."

She twirled once. "I do, don't I? I saw this gown at Iris's boutique and knew it was the one."

She stopped abruptly as if something about her words had surprised her, but she shook her head, laughed a bit and walked over to him, shimmering all the way.

"You look long and sleek, like a dangerous jungle cat."

"I like that." She eased his hands away from his bow tie and made short order of tying it. "Jungle cat. Maybe that can be your private pet name for me."

Everything seemed perfectly normal, perfectly logical, except for that one hiccup when she'd talked about her dress being the one. Yet he knew something was wrong. Her voice wasn't different. Her sense of humor was on target. She looked fabulous. She smelled even better…

But there was something in her eyes. A shadow. As if she were sad or maybe thinking too much.

"Are you okay?"

She grabbed a sparkly white handbag from the corner of their bed. "Never better."

He caught her hand and prevented her from leaving their room. "You would tell me if something was wrong, right?"

"When have I ever been able to keep my mouth shut?"

That was certainly true. She was the most honest woman he knew. It was why he loved her...

His brain stopped. Froze. A hundred happy moments with her raced through his mind. His heart swelled. His throat tightened with emotion—

No! He was not supposed to love her. That was not their deal.

Or was it? Couldn't he love someone he was having an affair with?

Maybe.

Wasn't that the reason they couldn't keep their hands off each other? The emotion that connected them?

He stifled a groan. The plan had not been to fall in love with her. He couldn't commit. Someday she'd need a commitment. They got along, but they did not mesh. He couldn't trust. She needed that closeness. Plus, she would be entering a whole new world. He had to stay where he was. They'd both known it from day one.

But he loved her.

Just the thought filled his chest with warmth and his brain with wonder.

He loved her.

She headed for their bedroom door and he followed her out, his heart thundering in his chest. They were going to part someday. That was the only reason he'd let them indulge their feelings. He knew there was a natural end to this, so they might as well enjoy what they had and at least have memories.

But it had backfired. Instead of enjoying the time they had together, enjoying her, he'd fallen in love.

He paused at the top of the stairs, not sure if he should be confused by the way things turned out or angry with himself. Finding no answer, he forced himself down the steps. He knew the drill. There was a difficult, confusing side to everything. Questions. Troubles. Work. Endings that weren't always happy.

Plus, all along he'd known they couldn't be together forever. So rather than panic, maybe this was simply phase two of enjoying what they had for as long as they had it.

Maybe that was it? Sure, he "loved" her. Why wouldn't he? She was funny and lovable. And for as long as their lives fit, he could enjoy the feeling.

That had to be it.

Because he wasn't the settling down kind. And he wouldn't hurt her by telling her he loved her, then letting the relationship end.

They rode to the event venue, a castle near a

moor. His grandmother being the sponsor of the event, she and his parents had gone an hour before and were probably standing in a receiving line near the ballroom entrance.

Limousines cruised up the circular drive, deposited their passengers and drove away. Jace got out first, helped Penny, then Charlotte.

Touching her hand, loving the way she looked in the long, smooth, shiny dress, he swallowed back a torrent of feelings. How right she was for him. How much he loved having her in his life. How different his vision of his old age became when he imagined her in it.

He stopped the last thought. Stomped it out with a ferocity that scared him. He'd had a vision of the future with another woman. He'd had a best friend. They had betrayed him. Mostly, Mary Beth had told him, because she'd moved on. What they'd had had been great, but it had a shelf life. *A shelf life.* As if he were a can of creamed corn.

But he understood what she meant. That was how life was. People changed, moved on. No matter how strong his feelings for Charlotte, they'd ebb. They'd mellow. And pretty soon they'd be gone.

So would Charlotte's.

Refusing to analyze why that thought made him impossibly sad, he took her hand and led her into the foyer and to the circular ballroom. Crowded with people, the black-and-white floors were nearly invisible. Waiters in white shirts and waistcoats over dark trousers served champagne. He took a glass for himself and one for Charlotte.

She glanced around. "Where did my mom go?"

"I heard her phone ring just as we got in the castle."

Charlotte sniffed a laugh. "Modern technology. Can't even go to a ball without somebody finding you."

He gripped her hand, turned her to face him. "Let's not worry about modern technology. Let's just have fun tonight."

"That was the plan, Skippy."

And she was back. His Charlotte. The one who made jokes while she looked at him the way Emily looked at Oliver. As if he was smarter, funnier, more interesting than he really was.

His chest tightened. Longing washed through him. The urge to trust her, to believe in something he was sure didn't last, rolled though him—

He ignored all of it. "Let's go find our seats."

They skirted conversation groups with him needing to stop periodically to talk to people who recognized him. He saw the family table, in the front of the room, with Leni and Nick and Nick's parents already seated at the table beside it. The table where Charlotte's mom would sit.

"You know, you never really told me that you came from money."

He stopped walking. "Does it matter?"

"You led me to believe you were a working stiff, just like me."

"I am a working stiff just like you."

"No. You're someone who works, even though he doesn't have to."

"I still work. And if you take your dad's money, you'll be wealthier than I'll ever be…and I'll bet you'll still work."

One of her eyebrows rose.

Not sure what that meant, he said, "We're not rare. Every life needs a purpose."

"True."

"Which also means your dad's money doesn't have to stop you from being who you are. Except that you might look at your life as having a bigger purpose."

She glanced around again. Jace's heart melted. She was more beautiful than any woman there, more accomplished, too, and somebody ninety percent of the people in the room would admire.

"I have actually been thinking along those lines. Maybe working with Leni to figure out how to dole out our dad's money so it does the most good."

His soul filled with hope for her. "Really?"

"Yes. All along I fought the obvious conclusion. Money changes things. But I didn't want to change, so I bucked a little. But now…" She caught his gaze. "Now I see how it all fits together."

It was clear from the expression in her eyes that

she also saw *him* slightly differently. She understood his business better. Understood he wasn't ruled by needing to make a profit but by a desire to keep people safe. And made the connection that with her new wealth that was how she should live her life, too.

He felt the click again. The knowledge that they weren't merely right for each other. They were like interconnecting pieces of a puzzle.

And suddenly he didn't want to fight it. Dear God. He wanted this. He wanted what Oliver and Emily had. He wanted a home, this wonderful woman, any children they might have…and a life.

His breath stuttered as the truth of that hit him. The past years, maybe even as far back as Afghanistan, he hadn't had life. He'd simply been living. Waiting to come home to Mary Beth, then totally submerged in pain when he returned to find her with someone else.

And now, Charlotte had awoken him. Made him see what he wanted. Showed him how he— how *they*—could have it.

"Excuse me, Mr. MacDonald."

The waiter brought him out of his reverie. "Yes?"

"There's a call for you in the white room."

"A *call* for me?"

"Yes, sir. Can I show you the way?"

"No. I'm fine. I know the way."

The waiter left and he turned to Charlotte. "I

have no idea who would be calling me here instead of on my cell."

"Maybe Seth Simon."

He laughed, then impulsively kissed her, filled with something he could neither define nor describe. Cautious, but curious. Wondering if he should tell her his conclusions or wait a few days or weeks to let everything settle.

"I'll keep it short."

"I'll go chat with Leni and Nick."

"Good idea."

He circumvented the crowds by walking to the back of the room and through a nearly invisible door used by staff. He strode down one hall, then another to the white room, a room in an area of the castle not available to the public.

He opened the door and froze. There on a Queen Anne chair, his head shaved and wearing dark-framed glasses, making him unrecognizable to anybody but someone who knew him very well, was Mark Hinton.

"I'm ready to announce to the world that I'm alive."

CHAPTER FOURTEEN

CHARLOTTE CHATTED WITH Leni and Nick for fifteen minutes, meeting his parents, who had flown to Scotland with them for the ball. When Bill and Lorraine led Jace's grandma, Jean, to the main table, she realized dinner was about to start and she needed to get to the main table with Jace's family.

Panic fluttered through her. Her mom had disappeared and now Jace was gone, too. She didn't want to miss whatever Scottish delicacy was about to be served, but she also couldn't let dinner start without her mom and the host's grandson.

She turned to Leni. "I'll be right back."

"Better hurry. Looks like things are about to get under way."

"I know. But Jace was going to the white room." She shook her head. "A waiter told him he had a call."

Leni's brow puckered. "A call? Who wouldn't call his cell?"

Ill at ease, Charlotte rose. "I know."

Nick rose. "Let me come with you."

Charlotte shook her head. "No. You stay. If everything's about to start, we shouldn't both miss it."

"Are you sure?"

"Yes. I'm fine. Jace probably doesn't realize the time."

Stopping to ask one of the staff for directions, she made her way to the white room. Her tight dress kept her from taking long strides and she could almost hear dinner being served without her, making her stomach protest.

Finally, she found the room. A tastefully etched plaque marked it as the White Room. The closed door gave her a moment of pause as she considered that perhaps Jace had finished his call and wasn't there anymore.

Still, rather than walk down the hall a second time, she opened the door and found Jace sitting with a tall, bald man. Black framed glasses sat on the round table in front of them. And when the man turned at the sound of the door opening, she saw his face.

His aristocratic nose, high cheekbones, strong chin. He might have shaved off his hair, but she'd seen enough pictures in her lifetime to recognize her father.

Her lungs stopped taking in air. Her mouth fell open.

Jace rose. "It's not what you think."

"I don't think anything." She'd been having kind thoughts about Mark Hinton since her talk with her mom. And suddenly here he was. Head shaved, glasses probably disguising his identity enough that he could use a fake name and fly anywhere he wanted in a private plane that landed on a private airstrip.

Son of a bitch. Her self-centered, selfish, mean-spirited father had faked his own death.

As confusion became anger, she turned to leave the room, needing to get the hell out of there before she said something she'd regret. Or, worse, *her father* would try to explain why he was alive when he was supposed to be dead.

Jace caught her arm. "You can't leave until you hear the whole story."

"Why? So I'll keep my mouth shut? The way I have to keep everything I see with you a secret?" She shook her head, then looked at the ceiling. "I am such an idiot."

"You're not an idiot. This is a complicated situation."

She glanced at her father, wearing a tux, obviously intending to attend the ball, as if nothing was wrong, as if nothing was off or amiss or weird about him disappearing for months.

"Complicated situation, my ass. He—" she nodded at her dad "—wanted something so he set things in motion to get it. And you—" she looked back at Jace "—obviously helped him."

"No! I didn't know. I suspected and called his private cell but he didn't answer. So, I told myself I was just imagining things."

"But you suspected?"

Jace ran his hand along his forehead as if warding off a headache. "I suspect a lot of things. I'm a bodyguard. That's part of my job."

"He didn't know." Her dad rose and approached her. "And I'm sorry I put everybody through this, but the real point is, I made a mistake not being in your life, the lives of all three of my kids. But I needed an opening, a way to ease the three of you into my world. I knew if I just walked into your life, asking for a chance to have a relationship, you'd reject me, and even if you didn't, you'd be overwhelmed by the money, the press, the bodyguards. This way, with you thinking you were inheriting instead of meeting me, you—"

"No!" She rounded on him. "I don't want to hear it. You abandoned me. Now, you've made a fool of me. And my mom." She stopped as a new area of concern hit her. "My God! What is my mom going to say!"

Then she remembered that her mom had been missing since they'd arrived. She'd gotten a phone call and disappeared. She'd insisted on staying at a hotel in New York, entertaining herself, being by herself—

She squeezed her eyes shut. "She knows, doesn't she?"

"Yes. I told her after Jace took you to New York. She met me there."

She faced Jace. He spread his hands helplessly. "I did not tell him we were in New York! I don't know how he knew."

Her father said, "I love your mother and I want her back in my life, too…"

She pressed her fingers to her temple. "Oh, my God. I can't even take this in."

She whirled around and raced toward the door.

Jace said, "Wait, Charlotte!"

She whipped around again. "No. You knew how I felt about my father. How could you have kept your suspicions to yourself? You didn't even give me a chance to consider that he might be alive, to mentally prepare for this—" She pointed at her dad. "I think that's proof where your loyalties lie and it's not with me."

She headed out of the room again, moving faster this time. She didn't care if she pulled the seams of her beautiful white gown. She just wanted the hell out of there without the pain of having to hear any more from her dad. Or Jace. No wonder he wouldn't even consider a real relationship. Deep down inside he probably knew her dad would show up and she'd be gobsmacked.

At the entrance, she told the doorman that she was with Jace MacDonald's party, leaving early, and would he please summon her car. Happy to help, he called Jace's driver.

She waited ten minutes, afraid Jace would catch her, then suddenly realizing he wouldn't. Like Seth Simon, her father was a lost soul. Taking care of him was part of the job Jace was so good at. Fixing awkward situations, helping lost souls, was what he did best.

He wouldn't come after her. She wasn't that important. She was a temporary fling.

The limo drove her to Grandma Jean's estate. In fifteen minutes, she'd packed and was in the backseat again, her luggage in the trunk. Instructing the driver to take her to the airport, she sat back against the seat, too angry to cry. She got a commercial flight to New York, stayed awake most of the trip and took a cab from the airport to Jace's condo.

She packed again, taking the clothes she'd brought from Pittsburgh and leaving everything she'd bought at Iris's on Jace's bed.

Then she headed to Pittsburgh. It wasn't until she was home, in her own shower, that she let herself cry.

But not for long. Angry with her father, she wouldn't cry over him. Accustomed to her mom loving her crazy, selfish father, she'd almost accepted that her mom probably didn't see the craziness of this whole mess.

And Jace…

She couldn't believe she'd trusted him.

* * *

Jace ran after Charlotte until he saw the family limo driving away and realized he'd never catch her. He threw his head back and groaned, watching her drive off. Then he made his way back to the white room.

He had an enormous PR problem on his hands.

"Do you really think you're just going to walk into that ballroom, dance with Penny and pretend the past few months haven't happened?"

"I don't see why not. I have a reputation for being quirky. I've also spent all those months on an island not calling anyone, not using the internet, just staying in the house I typically hide in. I'm done. I want to be among people again."

"I thought you said you needed this charade to get your kids together."

"I did."

"Yeah, well, your charade pretty much cost you Charlotte. She's never going to recover from this."

"Or trust you."

"What happens with me is irrelevant." Even as he said the words, he knew they weren't true. His ex might have done a number on him, but *he'd* hurt Charlotte. A woman he loved so much he hadn't even realized it was happening.

"Is it?"

That might be a good question, but this was none of Mark's business. "My job is to protect you and right now my instincts are screaming that you're announcing yourself the wrong way. I don't think Charlotte will call the press and tell them you're alive, but if she does…then what?"

"Then I hold a press conference."

"And what about the third heir? Exactly how to do you expect to have a conversation with the child we haven't yet found, with him or her knowing you faked your death?"

Mark ran his hands down his face. "There are complications that would arise and make that impossible."

"Make what impossible? A conversation?" Furious now, Jace said, "For once, why don't you tell me everything. Not pretend, not hint, not insinuate. Flat out tell me. So maybe I can help you."

Mark squeezed his eyes shut. "Because Danny Manelli is my son."

Jace fell to the chair behind him. "Oh, hell." He let his breath out in a long, slow stream, then said, "Why the devil did you make him the attorney for your estate?"

"I wanted him to see everything, to meet his sisters, to know everything before I popped into his life and told him one of his one-night stands resulted in a child."

"What?"

"My son has a child that he doesn't know about." Mark pulled in a long breath. "That's really what started this. I found out Danny had a child and absolutely couldn't let him go through life not knowing his own son the way I hadn't known mine."

Jace rose. "You'd better get your ass to New York tonight and set up a meeting with the partners at Waters, Waters and Montgomery as soon as you get there to explain all of this."

"What are you going to do?"

"As involved as I am with the estate, now that I've seen you and talked to you in person, I'm pretty sure I have to at least tell Danny, as attorney for the estate, that you're alive. I might also be duty bound to tell the authorities that you're alive. But I'll give you a day." Thinking it through, he took a long breath. "Because I shouldn't have to do any of that. You should. You should call Waters, Waters and Montgomery and let them tell you how you can announce you're alive without getting arrested for fraud or whatever law you broke faking your death."

"Jace, I didn't even go online the whole time I was supposedly lost. I could claim I didn't know the world assumed I was dead. If there are fines or costs, I'll pay them. Don't worry. I set it up so I won't get in trouble."

"You'd better hope."

Mark nodded. "I'm more concerned about my kids." After a brief pause, he said, "And what about Charlotte?"

"That's something you're going to have to figure out on your own."

"I'm not talking about me. I'm talking about you. She loves you."

Jace sniffed a laugh. "Yeah. She does. And I realized tonight I probably love her, too. But right now, she undoubtedly hates me."

"She needs you."

Jace slammed his hand on the table. "Do you listen to anything anybody tells you? This little charade of yours made it so she won't ever trust me again."

"But you are trustworthy, Jace. You always have been. You just need to talk to her, explain things."

Jace gaped at him. "Are you kidding me? She's not even going to let me in her door!"

"Go, anyway."

Jace squeezed his eyes shut. He wanted to. He could not see a future without her in it. But worse, he hated having her think he'd betrayed her. He hadn't. He *wouldn't*.

The news was filled with the astounding discovery that Mark Hinton was alive. At her desk in her office in Pittsburgh on Monday morning, Charlotte scoured every article to see if her name was mentioned.

Not once did she show up.

In the process of searching for her name, making sure she was being kept out of this mess, she unintentionally read her dad's explanation. His boat had wrecked. He'd gotten to an island. Not a lie. He'd stayed on the island where he had a tiny home, enjoying the privacy. Also not a lie because his nearest neighbor was miles away. Most didn't know who owned his house, or even that there was a house that far up the mountain.

He'd stayed off the internet. Didn't watch the news and in general simply did not know the world thought he was dead.

When asked how he felt about his heirs dipping into the estate, he'd happily announced that he was thrilled to have his children back in his life. That the unfortunate belief that he was dead had brought his family together and he was ecstatic. Anything he owned, they owned. There would be no more separation.

The partners at Waters, Waters and Montgomery had issued a statement that they were happy Mark was alive, but Danny Manelli had been unavailable for comment.

She stared at the paper, beside the stack of tabloids she'd read, for the first time in her life totally adrift. Her mom had called her and she'd made peace with the fact that she was in Mark's life for good. It had been what her mom wanted Charlotte's entire life. She'd be pretty selfish not to be happy for her mom and wish her well.

She groaned thinking about holidays. No matter

what kind of idiot Mark Hinton was…she would be eating Christmas dinner with him.

But none of the articles or interviews had talked about Jace.

Why would they? He was an employee. The background guy.

Such a weird combination of absolute loyalty for his clients and distance with everyone else.

She didn't want to miss him. But she did.

Didn't want to long for him, but Sunday night she'd ached for him.

She looked at the picture of her mom and Mark on the front page of the paper and shook her head. Her mom had waited forever for Mark to come to his senses. With no guarantees. No idea he'd one day change his mind. Just a strong, unmovable hope.

She'd say Jace didn't deserve that kind of hope. But Mark Hinton hadn't deserved it, either.

Still, her mother wasn't a world-class executive. She hadn't put her heart and soul into her career. She'd put them into Mark.

All her life, Charlotte had considered her mom a chump of sorts. And Charlotte didn't want to be a chump, waiting forever for a man who didn't know he wanted her.

But a part of her, the part that had loved Jace's wit, his strength, the way he let her be herself… That part of her wept and mourned, though it

seemed crazy to pine for a guy who'd kept reminding her what they had was temporary.

But she did.

Every damned hour of every damned day.

Still, one morning she knew she'd wake up and
he wouldn't be the first thing she thought of. He
wouldn't cross her mind when she got into her
truck or pulled up to a jobsite. She wouldn't remember him following her around, pretending
to be her assistant, the dinners he'd made or the
Broadway shows they'd seen.

She'd be Charlotte again. Single executive,
looking for "The One," even though she was fairly
certain she'd found him, and he hadn't wanted her.

CHAPTER FIFTEEN

JACE HAD HIS cleaning service change his sheets when he got home on Monday night, but he still smelled Charlotte on his pillow.

He'd thought and thought about everything she'd said the night of the ball in Scotland. He knew she believed he'd had a bigger part in Mark's charade than he had. Though he should be able to explain, the truth was he wasn't sure how. He'd never told her he loved her. He'd never given her any reason to believe he ever would. Now, suddenly, after her dad shows up and Jace *needed* her forgiveness, he was going to tell her he loved her? And think she would believe that he'd realized it ten minutes before Mark showed up and their world had exploded?

He'd spent Sunday working to ensure her name didn't appear in any of the press releases Waters, Waters and Montgomery issued and that Mark didn't mention her name at his press conference.

He managed the one thing Charlotte had always wanted but he'd believed she could have. He'd given her her life back.

At least for the past two days.

Tuesday morning, he walked into his office suite—a reception room, two offices used by whichever of his team leaders needed space, one long, utilitarian conference room and his huge office.

"Good morning, Patty."

"Good morning, Mr. MacDonald."

He picked up the mail. "I've told you repeatedly to call me Jace."

She perked up even more, though Jace wasn't sure how that was possible. "I like the formality of calling you Mr. MacDonald. You're the boss, the guy in charge, owner of everything we survey…"

"Patty, I can see the whole of Manhattan from the window behind you. I don't own everything I can survey."

She laughed. "Such a kidder."

He sighed and headed for his office. She meant well. And he was a grouch. Might as well own it.

"Wait, Mr. MacDonald—"

He closed his eyes, took a breath and said, "What?"

"There's a man in your office."

He faced her. "You probably should have told me that first."

She giggled. "Yeah. Probably. It's Mark Hinton."

He held back a groan. "This day just keeps getting better and better."

He strode into his office with ultramodern furniture in shades of beige and coral, and uncomfortable visitors' chairs so no one stayed too long. "What did you break now, Mark?"

Mark rose from one of the coral-colored chairs shaped like a scoop. "I've broken nothing. And, in fact, I think I'm finally beginning to fix things. Leni and her parents have totally accepted me."

On his way to his desk, he leafed through his mail. "Only because they are nice people. Charlotte hates you. Danny is humiliated. He thought he'd earned the position as attorney for your estate. To find out he was your son and being bamboozled mortified him."

"He'll come around. I have a plan."

Jace groaned. "I don't want to hear any more of your plans."

"That's fine. I'm not here to talk about Danny. I'm here to talk about Charlotte."

Jace sat. "I have a guy keeping an eye on her. No one in her face, but men investigating the people who come and go in her life." He looked Mark in the eye, communicating that he'd better not argue. "That's the best we can do without her noticing us."

To Jace's horror, Mark laughed. "Oh, if you're nebbing into her business, she's noticing. She simply hasn't pounced yet." He shook his head. "She's a pistol. I adore her."

Jace stared at him. "You're crazy. You know that?"

"Of course I know that. But I'm not crazy as much as eccentric. And maybe forced to do things that seem wrong because I had to protect myself and my family." He sat back and tried to get comfortable in the scoop chair designed to make him say his piece and get the hell out. "But now I have you. Your team is top-notch. You know when to step in or when to step back. Your guys guard without getting in the way." He smiled. "Which makes you also sort of responsible for me feeling it's okay to come out into the world again."

"Peachy." He stifled the urge to sigh heavily. "My staff and I are thrilled. Unless there's something specific you need, I'm busy."

"Well, there is a little something that I need to talk to you about."

Jace leaned back in his chair. *Here we go.*

"I hate what you did to Charlotte."

Jace bounced forward and almost across the desk. "What *I* did to Charlotte? You have got to be kidding."

"Not kidding. I know I was the perpetuator of the whole fake-my-death thing that infuriated her. But I didn't lure her to trust me, romance her and then drop her like a hot potato when things got tough."

"I didn't do that." But he had. Sort of. Not intentionally. And not so damned cut and dry. "It might have seemed like that, but that's not how it went." He'd been on the verge of telling Charlotte he loved her, wanted her in his life, when Mark had shown up.

Mark growled. "I don't care how it went. I want you to apologize to her. I want you to somehow make it right."

"There's nothing I can do to make it right. Everything I say to her is going to look like I made it up to get myself off the hook for not telling her I suspected you were still alive."

Mark finally rose. "Say it, anyway. Tell her the truth and she'll believe you."

He headed for the door. Jace stood up. "No, she's too much of an overthinker. She won't buy it."

Mark didn't even bother to turn around. "Yes. She will."

Little pinpricks of annoyance ran along Jace's skin. As if there was anything he could do…anything he could say…to make up for—

What?

He hadn't really deceived her. He'd simply not told her that he suspected her dad was alive. But he hadn't been in on Mark Hinton's plan.

And that night he would have told her he loved her—

He did love her. He missed her so much he ached for her.

And she wasn't the kind of woman to throw her lot in with someone she didn't truly care for. So right now, she was hurting, too.

And why?

Why?

He knew she loved him. And he loved her.

He was more than willing to trust her with everything—his life, his money, his heart...

And he knew that deep down she'd always trusted him.

But a trickle of fear ran through his veins. He thought of Mary Beth, thought of how clueless he'd been that she hadn't wanted him in her life anymore. What he and Charlotte had had been deep and profound, but also new and fragile.

He could blame Mark for ruining it, but his inbred honesty knew that was a copout. The emotion of the moment in Scotland would have carried him along, would have allowed him to say, *I love you*, and then bumble his way into what came next.

In the cold light of day, he loved her so much that he wasn't sure he wouldn't have lost her even if Mark hadn't shown up. Blaming Mark allowed him to skirt his real issues. What if everything they felt was smoke and mirrors, a temporary thing that would wither like the grass in winter?

Could he lose the real love of his life and survive? Or was it better to pretend Mark had ruined everything and not have to face the misery of hearing Charlotte tell him it was fun while it lasted but she wasn't as interested as she'd thought she was?

The knowledge that he was a coward washed through him. He sucked in a breath, squeezed his eyes shut.

How could he fall in love with someone after such a short time?

How could he think that love would last?

But the bigger question dwarfed both of those…

How would he survive this loss if he never tried to talk to her, to say his piece, to win her back?

Wednesday morning, at her desk, happily ripping apart the budget of a newbie, Charlotte heard a commotion up the hall, but she paid no attention. That wasn't her job. If the receptionist had an iffy visitor, she was to call security—

Crap! Why did she have to think the word *security*? Now, her brain would whip off into one of those tangents about Jace. At first, she'd think good riddance. Then she'd remember how silly he could be, how fun, how sexy.

And from there it was a short trip to remembering—

"Tell your receptionist it's okay for me to be here."

She blinked. That was his voice—

She looked up. And that was him, standing in her open doorway.

After the train of her thoughts she wouldn't be surprised if she'd conjured him or summoned him. Or maybe her thoughts had turned to him because he'd been in the building, on his way up the elevator, and her sixth sense about him had kicked in.

She automatically said, "It's okay, April. I know this guy."

But as April shook her head and walked off in a huff, Charlotte's spunk returned.

"If you're here to tell me my dad wants to see me, get out. We had a chat. I'm pretending he's the new guy my mom is dating. We may never fix the other stuff but at least I can be civil to him if my mom has a Memorial Day picnic."

"I'm not here to get you to see your dad."

"Okay, then, if you're here to tell me I need a bodyguard, you can save your breath. As you can see, I'm fine."

"You're fine because your name hasn't leaked. Right now, in New York somewhere, there's a smart reporter who is looking into everything there is to know about your mom because she and Mark are clearly an item. Nine chances out of ten, that reporter has already found you. She's just trying to figure out if there was a connection between Mark and your mom around the time of your conception. It's only going to take one credit card receipt for you to be outed."

"If she's got a suspicion, I'm surprised she hasn't published yet."

"A tabloid would have. This smart cookie probably works for the *Times*. She'll have all her ducks in a row and when she writes the story there will be no turning back for you."

She huffed, but her insides quaked. She wasn't afraid of a reporter. Wasn't afraid of the world discovering she was Mark Hinton's daughter. The man was a nut case. Most people who found out would feel sorry for her.

Jace caused her trembling. He looked gorgeously masculine in his jeans and T-shirt. No leather jacket on this warm May day. And boots. The man wasn't a cowboy, but he could wear a boot.

Unfortunately, he was here for her father. Or the family...whatever. There wasn't an estate anymore. There was just money and a crazy dad who clearly needed someone like Jace to organize for him.

She returned her attention to the really bad budget of the newbie. "Okay. I get it. I've been warned. You can go."

He stayed lounging in one of the two comfortable chairs in front of her desk.

He said nothing for so long that she growled. "What!"

"I miss you."

Her heart leaped but her brain shifted into fifth gear with reminders of how he'd kept her out of the loop about her dad, always told her he wasn't the settling down kind. She had three long days of getting over him under her belt. Did she want to let one arbitrary comment destroy all that?

"Get out."

He stayed put.

"I'm serious."

"I'm serious, too. I love you. I think I loved you from the second you tried to give me the heave-ho out of your construction trailer."

The memory rose, swift and clear. As if it was yesterday, she saw him in the black overcoat and mud-covered Italian loafers. It hurt her heart especially because he'd slid in the *I love you*. The words she'd longed to hear when they were together. The words she kept telling herself weren't coming.

"If the first time you say you love someone is in the middle of trying to get her back, it doesn't count. It could be a tactic."

He sighed. "Always thinking."

"It was not thinking that got me into this mess."

"Oh, we did a lot of thinking. A lot of wondering what it would be like to kiss and touch and finally make love. The way I see it, thinking got us into this mess."

"Okay. You agree it's a mess."

"What about life isn't a mess? Life's a complicated roller coaster. Things go our way sometimes. Things don't go our way others. It's up and down and crazy. That's why I want someone I can trust with me for every second of it."

Oh, he knew how to get to her. He'd made her picture it.

She stared at the budget screen, not seeing a word or a number. "You may be able to trust me. But as we both witnessed, I can't trust you."

"I'm here to tell you that you can."

She laughed, still refusing to look at him. She didn't want to see those dark sexy eyes. Didn't want them to lure her into something that was oh-so-wrong for her.

"Well, I say I can't trust you. And I'm ordering you out. If you don't leave, I'll call security."

To her disappointment, he sighed and rose. "Okay, I'll leave."

Her heart stuttered. She really, really did not want him to go. She wanted every word he said to be true. She wanted him to love her and she wanted to be able to trust him the way she had when they were in New York—

Her usually intelligent brain told her to call him back. To tell him she loved him, too. And wanted him in her life, which was so much better than needing him.

But she stared at the computer screen, her eyes filling with tears of confusion. How could she love a man who'd kept secrets? Who betrayed her?

Call him back.
Call him back.

No.

She said no in her brain, even as she glanced sideways at the door, but he wasn't on his way to the door. He was heading to her desk. He rounded it, caught the top of her chair and spun it around so she faced him. Then he slid one arm under her legs and the other around her back and lifted her out of her seat.

Her breath hitched. A laugh bubbled but couldn't come out over the screech of her protest. "What are you doing?"

"I'm taking you somewhere we can talk. Somewhere that you can't threaten to call security."

"Jace!"

He walked out the door, up the hall, into reception.

Everywhere he carried her, people rose from their desks, craned their necks, followed them, confused but also curious.

"Stop. You're making a spectacle."

"I don't care. I love you. We're talking this out."

April all but swooned.

Charlotte's heart did a little melting itself. Still, she was supposed to be angry with him…wasn't she?

He hit the down button for the elevator. The employees of Kaiser and Barclay stared at them.

"Isn't one of you going to save me?"

An accountant stepped forward. Jace laughed. "Seriously? I'm like three times your size." He caught Charlotte's gaze. "And I'll fight for my woman."

The melting of her heart became like a warm puddle of happiness.

The elevator came. They stepped in.

Someone yelled, "Security is on their way."

Jace said, "Tell them not to waste time coming up here. We'll be on the first floor before they get up this far."

The door closed. "You can put me down."

"Nope."

The feeling of being held by him, her arms looped around his neck—for safety, not because they wanted to be there—the scent of him invading her space, all hit her at once.

"This isn't funny."

"Of course it is. But that's how we are. I could have sent you eight million roses and you wouldn't have cared. You wanted me to make a big move? I've made it. I showed your entire company that I love you and will go to great measures to keep you. If you want to talk about trust, that's a conversation I'm willing to have. Maybe ground rules would help."

She laughed and playfully slapped his shoulder. "If we have to have ground rules to have a conversation, that's the definition of distrust."

He caught her gaze. "So, you admit there's an us?"

Her soul got on its knees and begged her not to

throw this away. To take the olive branch. To love him and trust he would love her.

"There's always been an us."

The elevator doors opened. Three blue-shirted security officers greeted them.

"Stand down," Charlotte said. "He's with me."

All three frowned.

"I'm her bodyguard," Jace said, grinning.

She shook her head. "I'm one of the Hinton heirs. My dad's the jackass who let everybody think he was dead."

Jace laughed.

"There. Let that little reporter from the *Times* chew on that."

"You're accepting who you are?"

"If I want you to be honest, I have to be honest, too. Especially if we're going to start something."

"Oh, we started something a long time ago," Jace said, stepping out of the elevator.

The security guards parted and made a way for them. One shook his head and headed off to the left. The other two gave them puzzled frowns.

"You can put me down."

"No, I think I like holding you."

"I think you like showing off your muscles."

"That, too."

She laughed. The automatic doors opened. Everybody in the lobby watched them go through and out onto the street. His SUV, black with tinted windows, was right outside the door.

"I see you brought the security mobile."

"Not denying who I am, either."

He set her down, opened the door for her. But she didn't slide inside. She studied his face for a few seconds, saw the sincerity, but also her guy. The One.

Her future suddenly stretched out before her, different, better than anything she'd ever imagined...even if Mark Hinton was her dad.

Her lips twitched, then rose. Then she leaned in and kissed Jace.

When she pulled back, he said, "A smart woman would have led with that."

She threw her head back and laughed. "This is going to be fun."

She got into the SUV, and as he closed her door, Jace said, "Count on it."

EPILOGUE

THAT CHRISTMAS EVE Jace and Charlotte walked down the Main Street of Leni's hometown—Mannington, Kansas—arm in arm, their boots kicking the fat fluffy flakes of snow piling up on the sidewalk.

"I feel like I'm in a Norman Rockwell painting."

Jace glanced around. Everything in his life was perfect. He had plenty of work for his crew. He'd learned how to relax. And he had the woman of his dreams. The right woman this time. Charlotte was wonderfully honest. And beautiful. And fun.

"Or maybe one of those Christmas movies."

She took a long drink of the crisp air. "My sister is a dynamo."

"That she is."

"Do you know she and Nick are building a skating rink?"

He laughed. "Doesn't surprise me. Nick's a pretty good skater. Leni actually competed."

"Nothing about Leni surprises me."

"She did get the whole family to *her* hometown for Christmas."

Charlotte's voice lowered to a whisper. "Not Danny."

"Not yet, but Christmas isn't actually until tomorrow," Jace corrected. Still, Danny had always been the wild card, the one whose life Mark had felt needed fixing enough that it was worth bringing all three of his kids out of hiding. The one who hated Mark meddling in his life.

But Leni and Charlotte had also started out disliking him. Charlotte still kept her distance, though she'd had some good times with Mark that summer when Jace talked her into going out with him and her mom on his fishing boat.

The whole family was learning that life wasn't black and white, good or bad.

It was what you made it.

And Charlotte loved what she was making of hers with Jace.

Big, strong, handsome Jace. Absolutely positively The One.

* * * * *